PINE GROVE MYSTERIES

VOLUME 2

DAISY LANDISH

Editing by Jessica McKenna
Cover by Daisy Landish

BEACHES AND TRAILS
PUBLISHING

BRUSH WITH DEATH

A COZY MYSTERY

CHAPTER
ONE

THE EARLY SUMMER morning sun cast a warm glow across the town of Pine Grove as Peter Myers walked down the street. His rescued Labrador, Sam, trotted by his side, tail wagging whenever anyone greeted Peter. Peter waved back at the townsfolk, his mind consumed with the suggestions his doctor had given him that morning.

After his parents passed away, he had moved back to the little town he had grown up in. Now, after a year of being back, he'd found himself part of the rhythm of the town.

Dr. Jessica Stern, the local veterinarian and Peter's girlfriend, waved at him as she led her newly adopted beagle, Charlie, out of her house on her way to the clinic.

"How did your appointment go?" she asked as the two of them stopped to allow the dogs to greet each other. Charlie's backend wagged hard as he licked Sam's face.

"Doc says I should take up a calming hobby," Peter answered. "Apparently, solving the mysteries around here doesn't count as 'calming,' although I suppose he has a point."

Jessica laughed. "I'm part of an amateur painter's class. It'd be fun to go together. Pine Grove's got enough scenery to inspire the next Monet, and we could count them as date nights."

She winked at him. Despite being retired, Peter found himself very busy in Pine Grove. Between his schedule and Jessica being the only vet in town, it was difficult for them to find time to spend together.

"Painting, huh?" Peter's eyebrow quirked up in amusement at the thought. "I can barely draw a straight line, Jess."

"Art's not about lines, it's about expression. Give it a shot." Jessica started walking again, tugging on Charlie's leash.

Sam quickly came to Peter's side, letting out a huff of breath as though relieved that Charlie's attention was elsewhere now. Sam was great with other animals, but Charlie's eagerness did tend to get a bit overwhelming.

"I think I'll do it," Peter decided.

Jessica laughed, the sound bright and easy. "Well, if you need a model for your paintings, Charlie here is quite the muse," she teased. "When he sits still, at least."

"I'll keep that in mind, though I was thinking more along the lines of landscapes. Less chance of them moving around," Peter bantered back, watching Sam and Charlie exchange curious sniffs.

"Either way, I'd love to see what you come up with. Pine Grove could use a little more culture," Jessica said, her eyes sparkling with a challenge. "Classes are on Wednesdays. You can find more information at Bell's Art Store."

Peter tipped his imaginary hat. "Then it's settled. I'll sign up. Prepare to be dazzled."

They arrived at the clinic. Peter gave Jessica a quick kiss, then waved as she headed to work. He had planned to drive up to Boston today, as he'd been volunteering his lawyer skills for a firm helping underprivileged people, but they weren't expecting him and he could use the time to get what he needed for this class.

Turning to Sam, he murmured, "Well, pal, let's see if we can add a splash of color to this town's palette."

Peter and Sam made their way down Main Street. The sidewalks were busy with the Monday morning crowd of people heading to work. The local police captain, Donnelly, passed Peter near the café and gave Sam a distrustful look. Even though the people of Pine Grove had come to realize Sam was more than just a pet for Peter, Donnelly held a special dislike for him. Though that might have more to do with his dislike of Peter than anything else.

"Captain," Peter said, nodding toward Donnelly.

"Myers. I hope you have a license for that mutt," Donnelly replied. It was his usual answer.

Peter only laughed as though it was a joke and continued on. The captain was just sore that Peter had solved more of the crimes around town in the last year than Donnelly had throughout all his tenure on the Pine Grove police force. He had been extra grumpy ever since he returned from a recent vacation to the Bahamas.

Bell's Art Store was a cozy shop nestled between the bakery and the hardware store. The bell above the door jingled cheerfully as Peter and Sam entered, causing Mrs. Martha Bell, a woman with a shock of silver hair, to look up from her knitting.

"Peter, to what do we owe the pleasure?" she asked, removing her glasses. She let them dangle from a chain around her neck.

"I'd like to sign up for an art class. The one on Wednesdays," he added, remembering what Jessica had said.

Martha hummed, her eyebrows arching in surprise. "Are you taking up painting, Peter?"

"Doctor's orders," he replied with a shrug. "I need to find a relaxing hobby."

Martha chuckled, her laugh a comforting sound like the crackling of a gentle fire. "I see. And you just happen to want the same class that Dr. Stern is in, do you?"

"An added bonus," Peter answered.

She led him through the aisles of colorful chaos, pointing out canvases, brushes, and paints. "The classes are drop-in so you don't have to sign up for anything, just bring your own paints and canvases. Let's start with the basics."

She hummed as she looked at the various art sets lining the walls. She selected one that had three eight-by-ten canvases, twenty-four tubes of acrylic paint, a pack of twenty brushes and a palette all included. The supplies were packed into a hard-covered case.

"This will be everything you need to get started. The Wednesday class is acrylics like this; if you want to try oils or watercolors it'll be other days."

"Wednesdays," Peter said firmly. "Acrylics are perfectly alright. What do you think, Sam?"

He held the kit down for Sam to sniff. Sam stuck his nose against it curiously then looked up at Peter with his large brown eyes.

"Woof!"

"Sam seems like he approves."

Martha laughed and stroked Sam's ears. "And he's welcome to join us on Wednesday, too. Art soothes the soul, they say, and who's to say that doesn't apply to dogs too?"

"Thank you, Martha."

As Peter set his purchase on the counter, Martha added a small sketchbook to the pile. "On the house, for your thoughts and doodles. Every artist needs one."

"Thanks," Peter said, paying for his supplies. "Who knows, maybe there's a hidden artist in me just waiting to come out."

"Or at least a few peaceful afternoons," Martha said, handing him the bag. "Enjoy the process, Peter."

With his new supplies in hand, Peter stepped back onto the street. Sam padded alongside him, enjoying the walk. The leaves danced in the gentle breeze, and Peter found himself already seeing the world a little differently – through the eyes of an artist. The trees were lush, the street dark in comparison, the sky a wonderful blue.

He glanced down at Sam, "Ready to paint our masterpiece, boy?"

Sam barked in response, as if to say, "Lead the way."

And with a new sense of purpose, Peter walked towards the promise of a peaceful hobby, unaware that his simple choice would soon paint him into the corner of a much larger picture.

CHAPTER
TWO

THE COMMUNITY CENTER'S art room was bright and airy, filled with the scent of fresh paint and the soft murmur of expectant students. Empty easels stood like silent sentinels around the perimeter, each one an untouched field of possibilities. Peter arrived early, Sam faithfully at his heels, carrying the new artist's kit under his arm.

Martha approached him, smiling widely. "Glad to see you, Peter. You can have this easel here. Just make sure you tie Sam to your chair. Lots of the artists bring their pets and we don't want them wandering."

Peter tied Sam's leash to the chair and patted his head. Sam yawned and laid down, resting his head on his paws. His brown eyes tracked Peter's movements with a mix of curiosity and calm. Peter set up his canvas and arranged his paints, nervous and excited.

The other students filtered in, a mix of elderly folks, middle-aged hobbyists, and a couple of teenagers. They greeted each other with the comfortable camaraderie of a small town. Jessica was one of the last ones to arrive. She claimed an easel next to Peter and grinned at him as she set up her spot.

"No Charlie?" Peter asked.

"Charlie is still much too excitable for art class," Jessica answered. "I'll pick him up from the clinic afterwards."

"Alright, everyone," Martha called out as the clock chimed, signaling the start of the class. "I'm putting a picture on the overhead for those of us who want to work off it. For you newcomers, let's begin with some basic strokes. Don't be afraid to let your brush dance across the canvas."

Peter dipped his brush into a blob of blue paint, his hand hesitating for a moment before he touched it to the canvas. The paint smeared awkwardly, nothing like the gentle stroke Martha had demonstrated. He grimaced and grabbed a wad of paper towel to wipe it off.

Jessica caught his hand before he could. "Don't give up before you've even started."

"It doesn't look right," Peter complained.

Jessica hummed, then mimicked his action on her own canvas. Though the two smears were almost identical, Peter somehow felt hers was more elegant. She smirked at him, a teasing sparkle in her eyes. It was as though she could read his thoughts.

"Keep going," she encouraged, painting another sweeping brushstroke. "Art's about expression, not perfection."

Peter nodded and turned back to his canvas.

The class continued, with Martha offering guidance and encouragement. Peter found himself relaxing, the stroke of his brush becoming more confident, the colors blending into something that, while not a masterpiece, was uniquely his.

As the class progressed, the room filled with the sounds of creativity – the swish of brushes, the opening and closing of paint tubes, and the occasional step back to evaluate their work. Peter concentrated on trying to capture the forms of the projected picture at the front of the class. Though Martha told him to ignore the fine detail for now, it was a difficult process.

Beside him, Jessica's painting was taking shape nicely, a swirl of green and blue hues that mirrored the beauty of summer in Pine Grove. She caught Peter looking and shot him a quick, proud grin.

At the end of the class, Martha walked around to see everyone's work. She paused at Peter's canvas, tilting her head. "You've got an interesting perspective, Peter. It's raw, but it's honest. I like that."

"Thanks, Martha. It's definitely... something," Peter said, unsure whether to be pleased or embarrassed. From his view, it looked more like flat blobs on the canvas. Though, when he stepped back and took a better look, he saw he'd done a good job with the lines of sky vs ground and the silhouettes of the trees.

As the students began to clean up, Jessica lingered beside Peter. "Not bad for a first-timer," she said. "Maybe Sam could give you a few pointers?"

Peter laughed, glancing at Sam, who was now up and wagging his tail, ready to go. "I think he's just happy I didn't paint him into a corner."

"Well, if you ever need a break from your newfound artistic career, you know where to find me," Jessica said, her voice light but sincere.

"I might take you up on that," Peter replied, a warmth in his chest that had nothing to do with the sun streaming through the windows.

As they left the community center together, Peter couldn't help but feel that, despite his initial reservations, painting might just be the hobby he needed. Little did he know, his brush with art was about to lead him into a brush with death.

Two months had passed since Peter's first foray into the world of painting, bringing Pine Grove into the heart of summertime. And with it came an art showcase Martha hosted for all her students. Those who wished could also include their pieces in a silent auction to raise money for the community center.

Peter arrived with a modest canvas under his arm, Sam trotting beside him. He had worked on the painting all week, a landscape of Pine Grove's rolling hills beneath a twilight sky. It wasn't going to win any awards, but it was his, and that made it special.

The community center was abuzz with excitement, adorned with an eclectic array of paintings for the local art showcase. The scent of hors d'oeuvres mingled with the subtle tang of acrylics and oils. Residents of Pine Grove mingled, dressed in their casual best, and admired the artwork displayed around the room.

"Peter, over here!" Jessica waved from a corner of the room, standing beside a table laid with snacks and drinks. She was wearing a simple dress that brought out the green in her eyes.

Peter walked over, placing his painting on an empty easel. "What do you think?" he asked, a hint of nervous anticipation in his voice.

Jessica studied the painting, her head tilting slightly. "It's beautiful, Peter. You've really captured the essence of Pine Grove," she said, her voice warm and encouraging.

Sam sat by Peter's feet, his tongue lolling out in a doggy smile as if he too was proud of Peter's achievement.

The room filled with chatter and laughter as more people arrived. The mayor gave a short speech welcoming everyone and praising the community's artistic spirit. As Peter mingled, he couldn't help but notice the varied reactions to the artwork – admiration, curiosity, and in some cases, thinly veiled criticism.

One piece, in particular, drew a crowd – a striking portrait with bold colors and an almost confrontational gaze. The artist, a local named Alan, stood beside it, basking in the attention.

"Quite the piece, huh?" Peter remarked to Jessica as they paused to look at it.

"Yes, it's certainly... commanding," Jessica replied, her eyes tracing the lines of the portrait. "Even though it's not my style, I certainly admire his technique."

As the evening wore on, Peter felt himself relaxing, enjoying the simple pleasure of being part of the community. He and Jessica admired the works on display and even Sam occasionally received pats and treats from the other guests.

The pleasant atmosphere was shattered when a commotion broke out near the center of the room. Peter rushed forward as Sam whined. Alan, the artist of the striking portrait, lay on the floor. A sheen of sweat glistened on his forehead as he groaned with pain.

Peter's old instincts kicked in. "Martha, call an ambulance," he said, projecting calm and authority in his voice. "Everyone else, back up. Give him some room."

He handed Jessica Sam's leash, then knelt beside the fallen man.

"Alan, can you hear me?"

Alan continued to groan. His eyes fluttered, but Peter was certain he wasn't aware of what was going on.

"I'm going to check your pulse," he said anyway. He took hold of Alan's wrist, and was surprised to find that his heartbeat was steady and strong. Not at all like he expected.

One of the other painters called out, "Is it a heart attack?"

"I don't know," Peter answered. "It doesn't seem to be. Alan?"

Another groan.

"Did anyone see what happened?" Jessica asked.

The same painter shook her head. "He was fine one minute, and then he just... fell."

As they waited for the ambulance, Peter's gaze swept the room, landing on the portrait that had drawn so much attention. Something about it seemed off, more than just the bold style. His mind, trained to notice the out-of-place, bookmarked the thought for later investigation.

The paramedics arrived and took over, rushing Alan to the hospital. The event quickly dissolved as the guests left, the evening's excitement turning to concern and whispers of speculation.

Peter stayed behind, helping to clean up and making sure Sam didn't sneak too many leftovers. As the last of the guests departed, Jessica walked over to him.

"Quite the night, huh?" she said, her expression a mix of worry and fatigue.

"Yeah," Peter replied, his eyes still on the spot where Alan had collapsed. "Something tells me this isn't just a simple case of overexcitement."

Jessica nodded, understanding the unspoken language of a man who had spent his life unraveling mysteries behind each crime. "If you need help figuring it out, you know where to find me."

With a final look around the now-empty room, Peter and Jessica left the community center, the echoes of the night's drama lingering in the air.

CHAPTER
THREE

THE MORNING after the art showcase, Peter returned to the community center to pick up his painting. Martha had phoned him last night with news that Alan had been released from the hospital. It appeared as though he'd suffered some bad indigestion and a minor concussion, but nothing to worry about

The air was crisp, cool for mid-summer, but that was why Peter had gotten up so early. He breathed in deeply, enjoying the serene beauty around him. Sam weaved around him, never tugging on the leash but still playing with the butterflies and flowers they passed.

As they approached the community center, Peter contemplated the events of the previous night. The building looked different in the daylight, its windows reflecting the clear blue sky, oblivious to the human drama that had unfolded within.

How could a simple case of indigestion cause a man to collapse as he had? The concussion was clearly from Alan falling to the floor, but what had caused him to pass out? Peter shook his head. Maybe there was something else going on that Alan hadn't chosen to share with Martha.

Inside, the aftermath of the event was still evident. Easels stood abandoned, some paintings left behind by their owners, perhaps in the rush to leave after Alan's collapse. Peter's own canvas leaned against the wall where he had left it, the twilight hills bathed in the morning light.

He was about to grab his painting when a low, ominous growl from Sam stopped him. The dog's ears were pinned back, his body tense. Peter followed Sam's gaze to the far corner of the room, where a door led to a small storage area.

"Easy, Sam," Peter murmured, but his own heart rate picked up as they moved cautiously towards the door.

With a deep breath, Peter opened the storage room door. The smell hit him first – a metallic tang that he knew all too well. Blood. And then he saw it, the body of a man sprawled on the floor among scattered art supplies, a dark pool expanding beneath him.

Alan.

This time, there was no doubt about his condition. Peter tied Sam's leash and approached cautiously.

"Woof," Sam barked, as though giving him a warning.

"I know, boy. There's nobody else here," Peter said. He knelt beside the body, careful to avoid the pool of blood and checked for a pulse. From how cold the body was, it was clear Alan had been dead for hours.

Sam whined softly. Peter retreated, his mind racing. He needed to call the police, but he also knew that once they arrived, the room would become a crime scene and Donnelly wouldn't allow him near it. Having witnessed the police captain's ineptitude for himself, he couldn't leave the matter in Donnelly's hands.

He scanned the room quickly. It was a mess of canvases, paints, and brushes, but nothing seemed obviously out of place. No sign of a struggle, no weapon that he could see. But when his gaze landed on a set of paintings stacked against the wall, one of them was smeared with what looked unmistakably like blood.

As Peter snapped a few pictures, Sam barked. Peter stepped out of the storage room, scanning the area. There was no sign of anyone else, but Sam's gaze was laser focused on the door. His fur stood on end as he growled. Peter closed the door behind him to preserve the scene and called the police station.

After reporting the crime, he called Jessica. "Jessica, it's Peter. I'm at the community center. Alan's been murdered."

"Murdered?" The shock in Jessica's voice was palpable. "But he was just taken to the hospital last night."

"I just found his body. There's no mistake."

"I'm on my way."

Peter met the police at the entrance, leading them to the body. Captain Donnelly's face paled at the sight of the body, but he quickly tried to assert his authority.

"Mr. Myers, I need to ask you to step outside. We'll handle this from here," Donnelly said, his voice a mix of nervousness and attempted professionalism. He pointed at Sam. "And take your dog with you. This is no place for an animal."

Peter complied, stepping back into the main hall. As he waited for Jessica to arrive, he looked again at his painting of the Pine Grove hills. It seemed naive now, a simple image that couldn't possibly capture the complexities and shadows of the town he called home. Sam pressed against his legs, looking up at him with worried brown eyes.

When Jessica arrived, her concern was evident. They stood together, watching as the police worked, both knowing that this was just the beginning. The community center, once a hub of creative energy, now lay under the heavy silence of a crime scene. Yellow tape crisscrossed the entrance, keeping the curious townsfolk at a respectful distance.

Peter and Jessica stood just outside the perimeter, watching as the police moved in and out of the building, gathering evidence and taking photos.

Captain Donnelly emerged from the center, a notebook in hand, his brow furrowed in concentration. He walked over to Peter and Jessica, his expression somber.

"Mr. Myers, Dr. Stern," he began, "I understand you two were at the event last night. I'm going to need to ask you a few questions."

Peter nodded. "Of course, Captain. Anything to help."

Donnelly led them away from the growing crowd, seeking a quieter spot to talk. He harrumphed at Sam but didn't comment on him. Sam stayed close to Peter.

"Mr. Myers, how did you find the body?" Donnelly asked, pen poised above his notebook.

"I was going to pick up my painting and Sam started to get agitated. He led me to the storage room where I found Alan," Peter explained, his voice steady despite the churn of emotions. "He must have smelled the blood."

Donnelly's eyes flickered to Sam suspiciously before he turned to Jessica. "Dr. Stern, can you account for your whereabouts last night after the event?"

Jessica's face was a mask of professionalism, but Peter could see the tension in her eyes. "After the event ended, I went straight home, Captain."

"And you, Myers? Did you also go straight home?"

"I stopped by the store and picked up some groceries first. Was Alan murdered last night?"

"The coroner will have to give a report before I know that." Donnelly sucked on the end of his pen, then glared at Peter. "And for once stay out of it, Mr. Myers. I am quite capable of handling this investigation without you. If you think of anything else, let me know."

As Donnelly walked away, Peter turned to Jessica. "This isn't right, Jess. Alan's collapse last night, and now this... There's a connection here, I can feel it."

Jessica nodded, her eyes scanning the building. "I agree. But we need more to go on. Maybe we should talk to some of the other artists, see if they noticed anything unusual."

Peter couldn't help but grin at her. "So, you want to join in the investigation as well?"

"Knowing you, you're already putting together a plan." Jessica rolled her eyes but still smiled at him. "So where do we start?"

Peter looked back at the community center, the morning's events replaying in his mind. "Let's start by speaking with the other art students. They might have seen something unusual last night."

They made their way back to the crowd, Peter's mind racing with questions. Who would want to harm Alan, and why? What secrets did the blood-stained paintings hold?

"It's going to be a messy case," he warned Jessica. "Are you sure you're up for it? Pine Grove might look peaceful on the surface, but beneath lay hidden depths we are only just beginning to explore."

"I'm in," Jessica said, her expression determined.

Peter took her hand and kissed it. "Let's get started, then."

Sam whined, as though he, too, was pledging to do his best with the investigation.

THE LOCAL CAFÉ, with its aromatic blend of coffee and pastries, was the perfect place to find some of the artists from the previous night's showcase. They dropped Sam off at Jessica's house first where Charlie was. Because the beagle still got over-excited with other dogs, they decided to put them in separate rooms until they came back. The two then headed for the café.

As Jessica and Peter entered the building, the bell above the door announced their arrival, and several heads turned in their direction. The tight-knit community of Pine Grove meant news traveled fast, and by now, everyone was aware of the tragedy.

They spotted a small group of fellow art students huddled around a corner table, their conversation hushed but intense. Peter recognized them from the class; each one had displayed their artwork at the showcase. He approached the table, Jessica's hand in his.

"Mind if we join you?" Peter asked, his tone friendly but with an underlying seriousness.

The students looked up, their expressions a mix of curiosity and apprehension. "Of course, Mr. Myers," one of them said, motioning to the empty chairs.

Peter and Jessica sat down. The café's ambient noise provided a discreet backdrop for the conversation that followed.

"We're trying to understand what happened to Alan," Peter began, his eyes scanning the group. "Did any of you notice anything unusual or out of the ordinary last night, or in the days leading up to the showcase?"

The students exchanged glances, as though they were all waiting for someone else to start. Finally, a young woman named Lilly spoke up. "Alan was... intense. Passionate about art, but he could be very critical. Not everyone took it well."

Another student, a tall young man with glasses, added, "Yeah, he had a dispute with Marcus Hemsway last week. Raised voices in the hallway. It was about the authenticity of some paintings, I think."

Jessica leaned in, her voice gentle but probing. "Did anything unusual happen during the class itself? Any new faces or unexpected visitors?"

"A couple weeks ago this guy came in and kept looking at all our paintings. Didn't do anything himself, though. After class, he pulled Alan aside," a third student chimed in. "It seemed to get pretty heated, but I don't know what it was about."

Peter nodded, making mental notes of each piece of information. "Thanks, everyone. If you think of anything else, let us know."

As they left the table, Peter felt the first threads of the mystery winding around his fingers. A critical student, an argument about authenticity, a heated discussion with a stranger – each was a piece of the puzzle, but how they fit together was still unclear.

Outside the café, Peter put his arm around Jessica's waist. "Looks like we've got our work cut out for us."

"Marcus Hemsway. I think I know where he lives," Jessica said. "Let's check on the dogs and then we can take my car to find him."

Peter nodded once. The quaint streets of Pine Grove, once a backdrop to Peter's peaceful retirement, now seemed to hold secrets at every turn. Just how many more mysteries would the town reveal to him?

CHAPTER
FOUR

MARCUS WAS KNOWN to frequent a studio on the outskirts of Pine Grove, a place where he could work in peace away from the town's prying eyes. As Peter and Jessica drove down the twisting roads, the scenery shifted from the charming downtown streets to the more secluded, wooded outskirts. Peter could see the draw to working out here. It certainly provided a great deal of visual stimulation.

The studio, a converted barn painted in an eclectic mix of bright colors, stood alone in a clearing surrounded by tall pines. They found Marcus outside, a cigarette dangling from his lips as he stared intently at a canvas. He was a rugged man, his hands and apron stained with paint, his eyes sharp and assessing. He looked up as they approached, his expression guarded.

"Marcus Hemsway?"

"That's me. What do you want?"

"I'm Peter Myers, and this is Dr. Jessica Stern. We need to talk to you about Alan," Peter said. Jessica glanced around, moving from Peter's side to get a better look at the surrounding area.

Marcus took a long drag from his cigarette before responding. "Alan, huh? What about him?"

"He was found at the community center this morning, dead," Peter revealed.

Jessica watched closely for Marcus's reaction. She and Peter had discussed something about how they would do this confrontation with Marcus on the way out here.

Shock and disbelief flickered across Marcus's face before settling into a grim acceptance. "Dead? That's... I didn't think..."

"You had an argument with him recently. About authenticity and forgeries?" Jessica interjected, her gaze steady. She folded her arms as she studied him.

Marcus sighed, flicking the cigarette to the ground and extinguishing it with his boot. "Yes, we argued. Alan thought some of my pieces were forgeries. He threatened to expose me, said he would ruin me. As though I would ever sully myself by copying other people's work."

Peter stepped closer.

"Did you see him at the showcase last night?" he asked, his voice firm.

Jessica always enjoyed watching Peter work. He has such a tight focus it made goosebumps rise on her arms. She could just imagine how impressive he was while he worked with the FBI as a lawyer.

"No, I wasn't there. I was here, working," Marcus replied, gesturing to the barn behind him. "You can ask anyone. I keep to myself, especially on busy nights like that."

Jessica's eyes wandered to the paintings scattered around the studio. "May we look at your work, Marcus?"

"I don't do forgeries," he snapped.

"Of course not," Jessica said, raising her hands. "Peter and I are part of Martha's amateur class, and I've heard a lot about your work."

Marcus narrowed his eyes suspiciously at her. With a reluctant nod, he led them inside the barn, where dozens of paintings lined the walls and filled every available space. His style was bold and colorful. It was filled with abstract images and sharp lines. The control of the brush needed for such a technique was impressive.

Peter stepped toward a set of paintings in the corner. He bent over them, studying them. Jessica trailed over behind him. She frowned; the foremost one looked strikingly like the one Alan had displayed. Both were of a colorful, angular barn. Jessica recognized it as one of the many barns in the surrounding area.

"You have a similar style to Alan's," Peter said.

Marcus huffed as he stomped over. "It's called Cubanism. Lots of artists use the same techniques. Just because we chose the same landscape doesn't mean that I copied him. I have my own style, my own vision."

Peter looked at Jessica. "What do you think?"

Jessica folded her arms, tilting her head this way and that as she studied the painting. "I'm only an amateur, but they aren't the same painting at all. Just look at these brushstrokes. It's the same barn and the same art movement, but very clearly painted by different artists."

"Thank you," Marcus grumbled. "I didn't kill Alan. I had no reason to. He could accuse me all he wanted, but he had no proof to back himself up with. He'd only make a fool of himself."

Peter nodded once. "Thank you for your time, Mr. Hemsway."

They headed back to the car. Once they were driving away, Peter pulled out his phone. Jessica glanced at him, shocked to find that he had managed to take photos of the canvases.

"What did you do that for?" she asked.

"He's hiding something. Something is off about these paintings," he answered. "I'm going to send them to Donnelly."

Jessica nodded, though she didn't understand the importance. Peter's expression was intense, which meant he was onto something. She had learned that he didn't always think to share his thought processes. Besides that, it would be best if she kept her own mind clear.

After Peter sent the pictures and his message, Donnelly called. "I told you not to go playing detective, Myers. This is a police matter."

"Captain—"

"No. Leave it alone." Donnelly hung up.

Peter rolled his eyes as he tucked his phone away. "Let's head back to café, shall we?"

"Ignoring the captain?" Jessica asked mildly.

Peter reached over and took her hand in his. "It's okay if you don't want to be part of this anymore."

She squeezed back. "Ah, but this is our date case. So. The café. What are we looking for there?"

"Information about that stranger that Alan had a fight with." Peter nodded once to himself. "The pieces are here. I just need to put them together."

CHAPTER
FIVE

THE CAFÉ WAS ALMOST empty when Jessica and Peter returned to it. The owner, a friendly woman named Diane, was behind the counter, arranging the displayed pastries with a smile.

"Peter, Jessica, what can I get for you two?" Diane asked, her warm demeanor a welcome presence.

"We're looking for information," Peter said, getting straight to the point. "Did you see anyone unfamiliar around the café last week, maybe someone who had a run-in with Alan?"

Diane paused, her brow furrowing as she thought back. "Now that you mention it, there was someone. A man I didn't recognize. He and Alan had words just outside. It got quite heated."

"Do you remember what he looked like? Anything that might help us find him?" Jessica asked, her green eyes keenly focused on Diane.

Peter couldn't help but be distracted by how beautiful she looked with that no-nonsense attitude.

"He was tall, dark-haired. Wore a leather jacket, I think. Drove off in a red sports car. Can't say I've seen him around town before or since," Diane replied. "Do you think he could be the killer?"

"We're looking into every angle," Peter said.

Diane nodded. "I'm glad you're on the case. I don't know what we'd do if we had to rely on... well, I shouldn't speak ill of our police force."

Peter exchanged a glance with Jessica. "Thanks, Diane. If he comes back, give us a call, okay?"

With a new lead to pursue, Peter and Jessica left the café and headed to the local police station to share the information with Captain Donnelly. The station was a small brick building, the blue and white police cars parked outside a sign of order in the peaceful town.

Inside, they found Donnelly at his desk, buried under a mountain of paperwork. He looked up as they approached, his expression annoyed.

"Back again, Myers? What is it this time?" Donnelly asked, a note of resignation in his voice.

"We got a description of a man who might be connected to Alan's death. They had a heated argument at the community center a few weeks ago and another outside the café last week," Peter explained. He relayed Diane's description.

Donnelly jotted down the details. "A red sports car, you said? That might be something we can trace. I'll get my guys on it."

"Thanks, Captain. We just want to get to the bottom of this," Jessica added. "And with you so busy, we're just trying to help."

Donnelly gave her a strained smile. "Er, of course. I am very busy. Thank you for the new lead."

As they left the station, the sun was setting, casting long shadows across the streets of Pine Grove. The day had brought them closer to understanding the circumstances of Alan's death, but the heart of the mystery still eluded them.

"I should take Sam home," Peter said. "He's been cooped up too long today."

Jessica nodded. "I'm going to take Charlie back to the community center. I've got a doggy class with him to help socialize him better. While I'm there, I'll speak with the staff and see if they remember anything useful."

"Be careful," Peter warned. "If there's any trouble, call me."

Jessica parked the car and kissed him lightly. "I will. Don't worry."

Peter collected Sam and headed back to his home on the outskirts of town. As he drove, the quiet streets of Pine Grove seemed to whisper secrets. Every friendly wave from a neighbor, every flicker of movement in the corner of his eye felt laden with potential meaning. Sam sat in the front seat, buckled in with a doggy seatbelt. He watched everything as it passed with an unusually solemn demeanor.

The mystery of Alan's death was like a painting itself, layers upon layers of detail and emotion, waiting to be uncovered. And Peter knew that he wouldn't rest until the final piece was revealed, restoring peace to the canvas of Pine Grove.

CHARLIE TUGGED ON THE LEASH, eager to get inside of the community center. The building was closed for the night other than this class. As she approached, she read a sign on the door stating that the doggy classes were cancelled for the day. Her shoulders slumped, but as she turned to leave, she caught sight of Earl, the janitor.

"Earl," she called, jogging over to him. Charlie raced with her, tail wagging excitedly.

The janitor looked up, a set of keys jangling at his belt. "Evening, Dr. Stern. Heard about the trouble. Terrible thing to happen," he said, his voice low and somber. He reached down to pet Charlie's velvety ears. "They're calling in professionals to clean up that mess. Good thing, too. I wouldn't know where to begin with all that blood."

"Yes, it really is terrible." Jessica shivered. She had seen a few of the images on Peter's phone. "Some of the art students said Alan had an argument with someone here a few weeks ago. Did you see anything?"

Earl nodded, his face creased in thought. "There was one fella. Dark hair, wearing a leather jacket. Didn't know him."

Jessica's stomach knotted. That was the same description Diane gave. "Do you know what they were arguing about?"

Earl shook his head. "No, but he was here looking around the day before the showcase, too, asking about Alan. Seemed keen on finding him, but Alan wasn't here at the time."

"Did this man say what he wanted with Alan?" Jessica probed further, her mind racing with possibilities.

"Not to me, no. But he had an air about him, like he wasn't here to admire the art, you know?" Earl replied, his expression troubled.

Jessica thanked Earl and left the community center, her thoughts swirling with the new information. The pieces were beginning to fit together, but the picture they formed was still incomplete. Charlie dragged behind her, disappointed to be leaving his new friend. Jessica laughed and gave him a pat, which earned her an excited tip-toe dance.

"Come on, Charles," she said. "Let's get home and tell Peter what we found out."

THE NEXT MORNING, Peter and Jessica met at the vet clinic to share their findings and plan their next move. Jessica had a busy day ahead of her. Charlie was excited to see Sam, and they let the two dogs into the fenced back yard to play as they went over everything they found.

"A mysterious stranger, a red sports car, and a possible motive tied to Alan's outspoken criticism of forgeries," Peter summarized, his brow furrowed in concentration.

"And don't forget the argument with Marcus about the authenticity of his paintings," Jessica added, her eyes sharp and focused. "There's a pattern here, but we're missing the why."

Peter knew they needed more concrete evidence, something to tie the disparate threads together. He pulled out his phone and started to move through the pictures he'd taken of Marcus's studio. If there was a forgery at the heart of this, perhaps a closer examination of the art itself would reveal something.

He paused on the one of the barn, the one that looked like Alan's. "There's still something about this that doesn't sit right."

Jessica leaned over. "Let me see."

He turned to show her, but as he did so, his phone started to ring.

"Peter, you need to come quick. That man you were asking about, the one with the red sports car... he's here." It was Diane from the café, her voice urgent.

"I'll be there soon," Peter said. He jumped to his feet and turned to Jessica. "Can someone hold down the fort and watch Sam for a bit?"

Jessica got to her feet. "Sure, I can spare an hour, but I need to get back for Mrs Pearson's bull-dog."

Peter gave Sam's lead to Jessica's assistant and ushered Jessica out the door.

CHAPTER
SIX

PETER AND JESSICA arrived at the café to find it unusually tense. The patrons were huddled at their tables, casting furtive glances toward a man seated alone at a corner booth. He was the very picture of the stranger Diane had described: tall, dark-haired, clad in a leather jacket, his eyes cold and watchful. Parked outside was a sleek red sports car, its presence in the small town as conspicuous as the man himself. If he wanted to stay under the radar, he was failing immensely.

Without hesitation, Peter approached the man, Jessica and a curious Sam following closely behind. The stranger looked up, his gaze measuring and guarded.

"Can I help you?" he asked, his voice smooth and confident.

"Peter Myers," Peter said, holding out his hand. "And this is Jessica Stern."

"Luke Wellington. What do you want?"

Peter didn't waver. "We believe you had some unfinished business with Alan."

Luke's expression remained unreadable, but there was a flicker of recognition in his eyes. "Alan was a fool. He meddled in things he didn't understand."

Peter leaned in, his eyes locked on the stranger. "So, you silenced him?"

Luke smirked, a hint of arrogance in his demeanor. "I didn't kill Alan, if that's what you're suggesting. But I won't pretend I'm mourning his loss."

Jessica interjected, her voice steady. "You mean because of his crusade against forgeries?"

"I don't know anything about forgeries."

Peter studied him and played on a hunch. "Do you think Marcus would say the same?"

Luke's smirk faded. He stood and threw a handful of bills on the table. "We're done here."

"Maybe we should go to the police with this information," Jessica threatened.

"By all means, do," Luke said, laughing as he shook his head. "I've seen Donnelly at work. I didn't touch Alan. Murder is a nasty business, not one that I'm going to mix myself up in. We had our differences, but they weren't the type to end in death."

He stalked from the café, the patrons and Diane watching him closely. Peter pulled on a glove from his pocket picked up the bills he'd left behind, checking them thoroughly. They seemed to be real, and was enough to cover the cost of his meal and a tip.

"Diane, do you have a clean plastic bag I can put this into?" he asked the owner. "I'd like to take this to the police, to see if they can get finger prints."

Diane nodded.

"You think he's in the system?" Jessica asked, pulling out her own wallet. She pulled out enough money to replace what they were taking and gave it to Diane in exchange for the bag.

"Maybe." Peter carefully placed the bills in the bag and sealed it. "One thing's for certain. We need to have another talk with Marcus."

THE EVENING WAS cool and quiet, a stark contrast to the intensity of the day's events, when Peter and Jessica arrived at Marcus's studio. The man himself was hard at work, his focus entirely on the canvas before him as he painted in swift brushstrokes. He looked up as they entered and wiped his hands on a rag, his expression wary.

Jessica stepped around Peter to take a closer look at the canvases Marcus had set up. Specifically, the ones that were similar to the painting that Alan had displayed at the community center.

"Back again?" Marcus said, his voice tinged with curiosity and caution. "I told you all I know. You should check out that guy Alan was arguing with."

Peter nodded. "We talked to him. He claims he didn't kill Alan but we think there's more to the story."

"Such as forgeries." Jessica picked up the work that most resembled Alan's. "Tell me, Marcus, did you do this one as proof of your skills for Luke?"

"I told you—"

"Something Peter pointed out made me think," she said, turning back to him. "The brushstrokes are very different from Alan's... but they're also very different from your usual ones. In fact, they're more similar to Juan Gris, the famous Cubanist painter."

She turned it around and gazed piercingly into Marcus's eyes.

"Luke wanted to see if you could copy not only style, but paint strokes as well," Peter said, folding his arms. "Alan found out what you were doing."

Marcus let out a long breath, his shoulders sagging slightly. "I never wanted any of this. I just wanted to make art, to be recognized for my work. But I was behind on my mortgage. I couldn't afford supplies. I needed money and quick."

Jessica stepped forward, setting the painting aside. "So, Luke did contract you for forgeries?"

Marcus hesitated, then motioned for them to follow him to a corner of the studio. He pulled back a tarp, revealing several canvases. With a resigned look, he pointed to them.

"These are the ones I've been working on. Alan... he suspected, but he didn't know. He saw my painting of that barn and accused me of copying him, but he didn't understand the full extent."

Jessica studied the paintings, the lines and colors telling a story of ambition and desperation.

"But you didn't kill him," Peter said.

"No," Marcus affirmed, his gaze steady. "I was angry, scared even, but I didn't kill him. And when I heard what happened, I knew things had gone too far."

Jessica placed a hand on Marcus's arm, her voice soft. "We believe you, Marcus. But we need your help to figure out who did."

Marcus nodded, a sense of relief washing over him. "Anything you need."

With Marcus's cooperation, they went over the timeline of events, the interactions with Alan, and Luke's involvement. Piece by piece, the story began to take shape, a tale of art, envy, and deceit.

As they left the studio, Jessica looked back at the canvases, a silent testament to the complex dance between creativity and ethics. The drive back to town was contemplative, both she and Peter lost in thought.

Back in Pine Grove, they decided their next step was to talk to the other local artists, anyone who might have had a grievance against Alan or a connection to the stranger. As they made their rounds, the picture became increasingly clear. Alan's vocal opposition to forgeries had made him enemies, and his determination to expose the truth had put him in danger.

But who had taken that final, fatal step? And why?

The answers were close, Jessica could feel it. Was this why Peter was always so determined to figure out these cases? It was a mix of apprehension and giddy excitement. She let out a long sigh as they returned to her home. Charlie started baying from inside the house as soon as they parked.

"Want to stay for dinner?"

"Thanks, that'd be great," Peter replied. He leaned over and kissed her lightly. "You're the best, you know that?"

Jessica laughed as she slipped from the car. "Oh, I don't know about that. You're pretty good yourself."

They headed into the house where Charlie was waiting, arms wrapped around each other. Despite the circumstances of their investigation, Jessica felt closer to Peter than she had before. Maybe they should investigate more cases together, after this one was over…

ARMED with new information and a clearer picture of the motives involved, Peter and Jessica decided to confront some of the local artists who had been particularly vocal in their criticism of Alan. They hoped that by understanding the relationships and rivalries within Pine Grove's art community, they could identify the person responsible for Alan's death.

Their first stop was the home of Evelyn, a well-respected painter known for her beautiful landscapes but also for her short temper and disdain for what she considered "lesser art." Her house was as colorful and vibrant as her paintings, with a wild garden full of sculptures and blooms.

Evelyn greeted them at the door, her expression one of mild annoyance. "Peter, Jessica, to what do I owe the pleasure?" she asked, her voice sharp.

"We're here about Alan," Peter said casually. "We know there was tension between the two of you. Can you tell us where you were the night he died?"

Evelyn's eyes narrowed, but she invited them in. "I was here, painting. I have no love for Alan, but I didn't kill him. He was a fool, but even I wouldn't wish death upon him."

As they spoke, Peter noticed a series of unfinished paintings in her studio, each one more aggressive than the last. "These are quite intense, Evelyn. A departure from your usual style."

Evelyn followed his gaze, a flash of defensiveness crossing her features. "Art is about evolution. I'm exploring new depths."

Jessica interjected, her tone gentle yet probing. "Did you have any contact with Luke Wellington? He had dealings with several artists in town."

Evelyn hesitated, then sighed. "He approached me, yes. Wanted me to be part of some scheme. I refused. My work stands on its own."

"Do you know of anyone else involved?" Peter asked.

Evelyn rubbed the back of her neck. "I'm not going to throw around accusations."

"So, you do know someone?" Jessica probed.

"That man has been all over town. Why don't you ask him instead of bothering me?" Evelyn snapped. It was clear she wanted them gone.

Peter stood. "Thank you for your time. We'll get out of your hair now."

Evelyn saw them to the door and slammed it shut behind them. As they walked away, Jessica turned to Peter. "What do you think?"

Peter looked back at the vibrant house, his mind racing. "I think we're getting closer. But we need something concrete, a final piece to tie it all together."

Determined to chase down every lead, they visited other artists, each one adding a piece to the complex puzzle of Alan's death. Accusations, resentments, and secrets spilled out, painting a picture of a community divided by ambition and fear. Martha was particularly forthcoming, explaining how she'd seen Luke talking with several other artists in her classes.

"I don't want to get anyone into trouble," she said. "But I did hear that stranger telling Alan to meet him at the community center after the showcase. Do you think he's the killer?"

"We don't have any suspects in mind yet," Peter said.

Jessica folded her arms, exhausted from the day's questioning. "All we know is that Marcus was working with Luke in his forgery scheme. At least, they were starting. I don't think it actually went anywhere yet."

Martha's eyes widened and she gasped. "Marcus? But... oh, dear! He was in the art shop earlier today, buying some new paint. I heard him say something about delivering the first batch tonight and then leaving. He and Luke must have killed Alan—and they're skipping town."

She clutched at her chest, trembling. Before they left, Martha handed them a flyer for the art showcase, Luke's contact details scrawled on the back. "He gave this to Alan last week," she said, unaware that it would lead them straight to Luke's door.

Peter growled under his breath as he headed for the door. "If there's something going down tonight, we'll catch them in the act."

Jessica raced after him, pulse hammering as they headed into the night. Pine Grove's sleepy streets belied the drama unfolding. As they drove toward Luke Wellington, Jessica felt her stomach twist into knots.

Were they about to unmask a killer?

CHAPTER
SEVEN

THE NIGHT WAS dark and still as Peter and Jessica made their way to the address linked to where Luke's red sports car had been seen parked outside. It was an isolated house on the outskirts of Pine Grove, surrounded by dense woods that seemed to watch in silence.

As they approached, the house loomed out of the darkness, its windows dark and unwelcoming. They parked a short distance away and approached on foot, their senses alert for any sign of movement.

Peter's hand lifted to the door, ready to knock, when it swung open. Standing in the doorway was Luke Wellington. His expression of surprise quickly turned to resignation.

"I've been expecting you," he said, stepping back to let them in.

The inside of the house was stark, the walls adorned with various pieces of art, some clearly valuable, others more obscure. The man led them to a sitting room where they could talk, his movements calm and deliberate.

"You're behind the forgeries," Peter stated, not bothering with pleasantries. "You had dealings with several artists in Pine Grove, but Alan found out about it and confronted you."

The man sighed, sinking into a chair. "I won't deny it. Art is a business, and forgery is just another part of it. But I didn't kill Alan. He was becoming a problem, yes, but murder? That's not my style. The forgeries I'd been getting here aren't that good. I'd just move to a new town."

"Then who did kill Alan?" Jessica asked, her voice steady.

The man looked at them, a hint of sadness in his eyes. "The art world is cutthroat. Alan made many enemies with his crusade. One of them decided to take matters into their own hands."

Peter leaned forward, his gaze piercing. "We need a name."

After a moment of hesitation, the man reached into his pocket and pulled out a piece of paper, sliding it across the table. "This is all I know. It's up to you to do the rest."

Peter picked up the paper, his eyes scanning the contents. It was a list of transactions and communications, all leading to one name—his heart sank. Was this true, or was Luke just trying to save his own skin?

"This can't be true," Jessica protested when she read the name.

"I was with Marcus Hemsway the night of the showcase. We were delivering some pieces up to Boston, and we didn't get back until after Alan's death," Luke continued. "I got a parking ticket that will prove it. The cop who ticketed me saw us both."

"We'll look into it," Peter said. "Don't leave town."

Luke shook his head. "Not planning on it, not until my name is cleared from this murder business."

They left the house, the night suddenly feeling colder, the truth heavier. As they drove back towards town, Peter's mind raced with the implications of what they had learned.

They went straight to the police station, where they found Captain Donnelly and presented him with the evidence. Donnelly's eyes widened as he read the name, a mixture of shock and understanding crossing his face.

"Luke Wellington's alibi needs to be checked out," Peter said.

Donnelly nodded. "We'll take it from here," he said, already reaching for his phone to issue orders.

Peter and Jessica stepped outside, the station's fluorescent lights casting long shadows on the pavement. They looked at each other, the weight of the case settling between them.

"We did it, Jess," Peter said, a weary smile on his lips.

"So, you think Luke was telling the truth? About the killer?"

"I do."

Jessica sighed as she leaned into his side. As they walked back to the car, the stars overhead seemed to watch in silent judgment, the secrets of Pine Grove laid bare. They knew that the town would never be the same, that the shadows once hidden were now part of its story.

But for now, there was a sense of closure, a sense that justice would be served. And as they drove away, leaving the police station behind, they knew that whatever the future held, they would face it together.

IN THE DAYS THAT FOLLOWED, Pine Grove buzzed with the news of the arrest of Martha Bell. Once admired in the local art scene, she was now being charged with Alan's murder. The evidence Peter and Jessica had helped uncover painted a clear picture of jealousy, fear, and desperation that had led to a fatal decision.

Martha had been the first person Luke approached for his forgery scheme and she'd jumped onto the opportunity, then used her free classes to teach others the same techniques. She directed him toward the most promising students and tricked them into thinking that it was all above board... until Alan figured it out.

She would have lost everything if her crimes had come to light, and she killed him to keep him silent.

The community was shaken, the idyllic veneer of the town cracked by the revelation of what one of its own was capable of. Yet, there was also a sense of relief, a feeling that justice was being served and that perhaps the town could find its way back to peace.

Peter and Jessica found themselves at the heart of it all, their roles in solving the case the subject of quiet nods and respectful whispers. They met at the café, now returning to its role as the central hub of town life, to discuss the case's resolution.

The case might have been solved, but the experience had changed them. They had delved into the darkest corners of their town and come out the other side, their bond stronger and their commitment to Pine Grove deeper.

As they finished their drinks, Jessica turned to Peter. "What now? Back to painting?"

Peter chuckled, glancing at the sketchbook he had begun to fill with the vibrant scenes of Pine Grove. "Maybe. It's a peaceful hobby, after all."

They stood up, leaving the café to the sound of the bell above the door. Outside, the town went about its business, the rhythm of life continuing unabated. Children played in the park, shopkeepers greeted their customers, and the trees whispered secrets in the breeze.

Peter and Jessica walked together, their steps in sync, Sam and Charlie trotting beside them. They knew there would be other mysteries, other challenges to face. But for now, they were content to enjoy the moment, the quiet victory of justice served and peace restored.

And as they walked, the sun broke through the clouds, casting Pine Grove in a warm, golden light, a promise of brighter days to come.

CHAPTER
EIGHT

THE SUMMER WAS in full swing in Pine Grove, the town alive with the vibrant colors and activities of the season. The sun hung high in the sky, casting a warm glow over the streets and houses, and the air was filled with the sounds of laughter and life.

Peter sat on his porch in the early evening, the day cooling into a pleasant, balmy night. As he contemplated the canvas before him, he sipped a cold lemonade, enjoying the quiet moment of reflection. Sam lay at his feet, panting softly, content in the company of his owner and the gentle evening breeze.

The recent events in Pine Grove, culminating in the resolution of Alan's case, seemed like a distant memory in the light of these peaceful summer evenings. The town had shown its resilience, coming together in the face of adversity, and now it basked in the calm after the storm.

The vibrant green of summer had enveloped Pine Grove, the town basking in the warmth and energy of the season. Flowers bloomed in every garden, and the laughter of children playing in the park filled the air. The longer days and clear blue skies seemed to infuse the town with a renewed sense of life and possibility.

Out on his property, away from town, Peter felt the tranquility of the coming night. Sounds of sleepy animals came from the forest adjacent to his property, preparing for the night. He dipped his brush into a palette of bright, summer colors, the image on the canvas slowly taking form.

As he painted, Jessica pulled up in her car. She got out, carrying a basket with her. Charlie trotted at her side. Though the beagle wiggled with excitement, he kept a close eye on Jessica and never left the 'heel' position.

"I thought we might like the day-olds that Diane sells cheap," she announced, setting the basket on the table.

"Thanks." Peter glanced down at Sam, who gazed back at him. "Go play."

"Woof!" Sam barked excitedly, then tore off. When they had all this space to race about in, he really did enjoy Charlie's presence.

As the dogs played, Jessica leaned in to look at Peter's canvas. "You've really embraced this, Peter. I love the way you captured the light and shadows of a summer day."

Peter stepped back, appraising his work. "It's become a part of my routine now. It helps me see the beauty of Pine Grove in a new light."

Jessica nodded, her gaze following the curves and colors of his painting. "It's wonderful. You've captured the essence of summer here."

They sat together, sharing pastries and stories, the bond between them strengthened by the experiences they had shared. Sam and Charlie romped and rolled in the yard, and the conversation turned to the Summer Festival that the mayor had decided to hold for Pine Grove.

"The whole town is buzzing about it," Jessica said. "It's going to be a celebration of everything we love about Pine Grove."

Peter nodded in agreement. "It's exactly what we need—a chance to come together and enjoy the best of what our town has to offer. It's about community, about finding joy in the simple things, and about being there for each other."

Jessica nodded, her hand finding its way into his. "It's times like these that remind me why I love this place so much."

As the sky darkened and the first stars appeared, lanterns and fairy lights in the surrounding gardens twinkled to life, casting a soft glow around them.

In the comfort of the evening, with the town they loved so much surrounding them, Peter and Jessica knew that they were exactly where they were meant to be. The summer festival would be a new chapter for Pine Grove, a time to celebrate, to heal, and to look forward to the future with hope and anticipation.

The End.

FROZEN WITH FEAR

A COZY MYSTERY

PROLOGUE

PETER MYERS MOVED to Pine Grove five years ago, following retirement from his work with the FBI and a divorce. A divorce which, looking back, could have gone better. That said, it could have gone worse. The one thing Peter thought he and his ex-wife did well was not pull the kids into their problems. Now, on a warm summer evening, he sat down at the familiar café with Rina, his daughter, Matt, his son, and Jessica, his girlfriend.

"It's so lovely to meet you both," Jessica said with a smile.

Dr. Jessica Stern was Pine Grove's veterinarian. They'd met when Peter found his dog, Sam, wandering in the woods. These days, Jessica had a rescued beagle. The two dogs had become fast friends and were currently chilling under the table.

Rina gave Jessica a big smile. "It's good to meet you, too... finally," she added with a playfully sour look at Peter. "Matt and I were talking about it on the drive out here. You've been helping our father solve mysteries for five years now and he's never introduced you."

"It's only been recently that things have become... serious enough for introductions," Jessica said, giving Peter a smile.

Peter nodded. "How are both of you doing in New York?"

"Pretty good," Matt said. He grinned. "I proposed to Sidney. We're going to get married next year. I wanted to bring him along, but his work is slammed right now."

"Wow! Congratulations," Peter cried. "That's cause for celebration. After dinner, we'll open up a bottle of champagne at home."

Rina slugged Matt's arm. "Ha! I knew it. Which is one of the reasons it'll be so much easier for me to move. I won't have to look after you anymore."

Matt frowned at her.

Well, this was a relief. Peter had been worried that introducing his kids to his first serious relationship since the divorce would be awkward. But they were acting like themselves. He ought to have known better. He had good kids. It was one thing he and his ex still agreed on.

"Where are you moving to?" Peter asked Rina.

"Don't know yet." Rina shrugged. "I have a few possibilities. But let's talk wedding! Do you and Sidney have any sort of theme? Are you going to wear tuxes or something less traditional?"

Matt held up his hands, laughing. "Whoa, whoa! It's just happened. We haven't made any plans and I don't want tonight to end up all about me. I was hoping to be overshadowed by your moving plans," he added with a wry shake of his head. "You know I don't like a lot of attention."

Jessica shared a glance with Peter. "Sounds like someone I know."

"You'll find we're all like that," Rina said, leaning forward. "Even those of us who are attention seekers don't like it once we have the attention we seek. Which means we have to put you two into the spotlight! I heard that the Erik Lang murder trial has finally closed."

Peter shook his head at the way Rina could flit from one topic to another so easily. If this wasn't normal for her, he would have considered it a sign that she was uncomfortable with the current situation. That was just how she was, though.

"Erik Lang. That was a long time ago," Jessica said.

"You two worked that case together, right?" Matt asked, leaning forward slightly.

Peter and Jessica exchanged another look. They'd been caught.

There was no way to deflect from this conversation without being terribly obvious about it. Oh, well. It just meant he'd have to ambush his kids about questions of their lives later.

"We did," Peter confirmed. He leaned back in his chair. "It was during the winter festival four years ago."

CHAPTER
ONE

FEBRUARY IS ALWAYS a difficult time of year in those parts where winter still lingers. After so many months of cold, snowy weather, February is at the point where you have already endured for what seems like forever, while it's not yet close enough to spring to see an end to wintertime. At least, that's how it was in Pine Grove in New England.

As such, it was the policy of the town to hold its annual Winter Carnival in February, to give something to lighten the hearts of the town and brighten their spirits. Peter thought it was a good choice, although the weather was unpredictable enough that sometimes the festivities had to be moved indoors.

This year, the centerpiece of the festival was a beautiful ice sculpture maze. In summer, it was a hedgerow maze. Ice sculptures had been placed throughout the maze next to hot chocolate stands. It was the talk of the town, and Peter was looking forward to it. The deep cold of winter seemed a bit brighter when considering the hedges wrapped in burlap and covered with fairy lights.

Most of all, he looked forward to inspecting the artwork of famed local artist Erik Lang up close. He'd been a fan of Erik's work, but he worked solely in ice sculpting; his work was so delicate that it was also rather exclusive.

He made sure that Sam's boots were firmly on his feet before letting him out of the car. Sam at first shook his feet, but once the warmth of the car wore off, he stopped. Peter knelt beside him, doing up his winter coat. He'd never realized before how important it was for animals to be dressed for the weather. He had grown up without pets and despite his children begging for a dog, they'd only had goldfish, hamsters, and cats. He'd never lived anywhere where he could have a dog.

Sam might have a fur coat, but it was a thin coat; too thin for this sort of weather.

As Peter straightened, he caught sight of Jessica Stern at a booth near the entrance of the maze. A large sculpture was hidden under a sheet next to the booth. Peter studied the shape for a moment, but he was too distracted by Jessica to make a guess as to what the sculpture actually was.

He made his way to the booth. It was about the local animal shelter, explaining where they were, what they did, and how people could help out. It also had a few animals on display who were available for adoption.

"Hey," he greeted. "Thanks again for helping me out with Sam. That trainer you put me onto has been doing wonders. Sam's making leaps and bounds."

Jessica grinned back at him. "I'm glad to hear it. Mind if I get him a treat?"

Sam's ears perked up at the 't-word.' "Woof!" he barked.

Both Jessica and Peter laughed. Peter nodded at her. "Sure, go ahead. He seems excited."

Jessica gave Sam a dog biscuit. He gave a polite 'woof' in thanks and started to snack on it.

"Are you going through the maze?" Peter asked. "I hope you have someone who can take over the booth for you."

"Oh, yes. I'm actually not on 'booth duty' at all today. I just volunteered to watch over it while my friend ran home quick to get a warmer coat," Jessica explained. "Once she's back, do you want to go through the maze together?"

Peter grinned. "You read my mind. I was going to ask if you wanted to."

"That sounds wonderful! It should be opening soon. I heard the mayor talking with her aide, and they're just waiting for Erik Lang to show up." Jessica rested her elbows on the booth. "It's a beautiful day for it, with this clear weather and bright sun."

Peter was just about to agree when suddenly Sam growled. His fur stood on end as he strained against the leash, sniffing at the base of the big, covered sculpture.

"What's wrong, boy?" Peter asked, letting Sam pull him over.

The dog sniffed at the sculpture and growled again, then whined. His ears were lifted, his tail pointed straight and stiff. He pawed at the covering, then looked back at Peter. His eyes were big and he licked his lips. All of these were signs the trainer had taught Peter to watch for; they indicated Sam was under stress.

Moving cautiously, Peter lifted the edge of the sculpture. There was a suspicious red streak in the ice. His heart dropped as he quickly lifted the sheet up, blocking it from the public. He didn't want to cause a panic if he was right about this.

"Um, I'm pretty sure we're supposed to wait until the grand unveiling," Jessica said, sounding confused.

The grim discovery of a body encased in the ice dulled his ears. Peter mentally groaned. A streak of blood ran through the ice, ending at the base where Sam was currently sniffing. The ice was too thick to get a good look at the person's face, but it was clearly a real person. If it was fake, Erik Lang had a really sick sense of humor. The trouble was, how did a person end up in an ice sculpture?

Peter tugged on the leash, pulling Sam away. This wasn't his job anymore. He'd retired for a reason, and that was because he didn't want to be involved in all this grisly business anymore. He had his old family home to fix up and a dog to take care of. If he got too bored, he could look into giving pilot lessons.

"What is it?" Jessica asked. She had left the animal shelter booth. "You look like you saw a ghost."

"Almost," Peter said.

Jessica's eyes widened. "What are you saying?"

"There's a body in the ice sculpture. I'm going to call Captain Richard Donnelly," he said, pulling out his phone. "You go find the mayor and inform her. We're going to need crowd control and to lock down the scene at once."

CHAPTER
TWO

PETER TOOK Sam back home while Captain Donnelly removed the ice sculpture from the scene. Sam wasn't too happy about being left out of the excitement, but when Peter put on a slideshow of fire hydrants on the TV, Sam settled on the couch and watched avidly. Peter took the opportunity to put up the pet gate he'd gotten to keep Sam from chewing on cables.

Then he went back to town. He arrived at the police station to find Jessica was already there. He was surprised to see her. Why would Captain Donnelly want to talk with a vet?

"Oh, it's you," Donnelly said grumpily when Peter stepped in.

"I thought you might need my statement, considering I'm the one who found the body," Peter said. Donnelly had been rather antagonistic toward him ever since Peter had been the one who discovered a mob-related kidnapping when he first moved to Pine Grove.

"No need, Dr. Stern was covering it," Donnelly answered. "The body in the ice is Erik Lang. I talked with the man last night so we know that he died sometime after that, but with enough time for the sculpture to freeze."

Peter frowned. "How could there be enough time to carve the ice as well?"

Donnelly shook his head. "Lang didn't carve his ice sculptures. He carved the originals out of soap or clay or something like that, then created a mold he used to freeze the ice in. He must have hit his head and fell into the mold before it was done freezing. A tragic accident through and through."

That didn't make any sense at all. Before Peter could point that out, though, Jessica cleared her throat.

"Captain, even if that were the case, someone would have had to unmold the ice and put it in the maze. They couldn't have possibly missed a body in the ice when they did it," she said, brushing her hair behind her ear.

Donnelly frowned at her. "What are you saying?"

"Just that it doesn't look like it could be an accident," she said. "Maybe someone was hoping to make a statement by having the body found in such a fashion? If they wanted it to look like an accident, then the better thing to do would have been to leave it in Erik's freezer. Instead, we have this huge drama around it."

"I... huh." Donnelly rubbed his chin.

Peter stepped forward. He had to handle this carefully, so Donnelly didn't think he was trying to step on his toes. "I've heard in town that you're low on manpower right now. Is there anything I can do to help? I noticed there were several cameras around the maze. I could go to those businesses and ask for the footage so you can concentrate on compiling a list of suspects."

His hope to mend bridges was quickly dashed. Captain Donnelly gave him a furious look. "What, you think I can't do that myself?"

"Not at all. I just thought I could volunteer to take some of the grunt work off your plate is all," Peter said, lifting his hands.

"Look here, Myer," Donnelly grunted as he poked a thick finger into Peter's chest—he had the thick, strong hands of a farmer—and glared at him. "I know you're some fancy shmuck from the big city, but if you want to get your nose in police business, think again. I know all about your father and his mob connections. I'm not letting you get your grubby hands on this town, you hear?"

Peter bit back on the surge of anger that went through him. He'd only recently learned that his father had been involved with the mob. It was something he was still struggling to fully understand himself.

"There was no murder," Donnelly continued, this time turning to Jessica. "It was just an accident. I'll bet that the movers thought it was some sort of holiday goo in there. You could hardly tell it was a person, and when it's freshly unmolded there's this frosting that happens on the outside."

Peter nodded once. It appeared that he had no choice but to get himself involved in the matter. Internally, he was still seething. It was fair enough that Donnelly didn't trust him because of his father's connections. Peter had been on Donnelly's side of things often enough.

But to blatantly refuse to see that a murder had taken place? No. If Donnelly wasn't going to take this seriously, Peter had no choice but to step in.

He didn't realize Jessica followed him until he had left the police station. Footsteps followed after him and Peter whirled, thinking Donnelly had followed him for some reason. Instead, he found himself face-to-face with Jessica. She jumped back, and for a second, Peter thought it was because his glare had frightened her.

"Oops," Jessica cried. "I nearly ran into you."

Peter took a deep breath to calm himself. "Sorry. I wasn't paying attention."

"It's okay." Jessica shrugged. "Are you okay?"

"I..."

Jessica waited a moment, then sighed. "Donnelly seems to be barking up the wrong tree. I don't want to see this case end up unsolved because he's got some sort of beef against you. Where do we start?"

A rush of gratitude went through Peter. Jessica wasn't going to pry. "Let's start with talking to potential witnesses. When did you arrive at the maze?"

"It was close to eight," Jessica said. "Not many people were around, but I saw Leah Peabody."

Peter nodded. They found Leah still at the maze, arguing with one of the organizers that she still should be allowed to go through the maze. Peter managed to pry her away and asked her what time she arrived.

"I was here at seven-thirty, waiting to get in there. I'm not leaving until I see it," Leah said, gesturing angrily at the maze. "This is the only thing I've had to look forward to for two months!"

"Did you see anything strange?" Peter asked.

Leah shook her head. "Not today. But yesterday when I was checking Erik Lang out at the grocery store, that crazy Jordan Halloway started yelling at him. Held up the line for ten minutes and guess who the manager yelled at?" Leah glared at the maze operator. "Hey, you got a gun? Maybe you can get them to let me see the maze."

CHAPTER
THREE

JORDAN HALLOWAY WAS a wisp of a woman who owned Halloway Apothecary and Café, which was a store near the outskirts of Pine Grove. Peter had passed it before and always thought it seemed a bit… snooty. There was nothing wrong with having a higher-end store, of course. The big sign in the window that read, 'Loiterers will be prosecuted' and the giant spikes on the sidewalk just under the eaves, preventing people from taking shelter on stormy days, left him with a rather dim impression of the place.

Inside smelled of baked goods and essential oils. It was a mix that left Peter's eyes watering the moment he stepped into the place.

"Hello," Jordan greeted. She sat behind the counter, working on some sort of macramé project. Her lips twitched into the approximation of a smile as Peter and Jessica approached. "What can I get for you today?"

"I'm Jessica Stern and this is Peter Myers," Jessica said. "Can we ask you a few questions?"

Peter admired the way she took charge so easily.

"I'm Jordan and this here," she pointed to a young man sweeping the floor, "is Nolan Grimm. What sort of questions do you have? We have our organic teas on sale."

"We're looking into the death of Erik Lang," Peter answered.

Jordan's eyes widened. "Oh, really? I thought Captain Donnelly said it was an accident."

"He did, but we have suspicions," Peter said. "As I used to work with the FBI, I thought we would lend the Captain a hand. Forgive me for asking, but did you have any issues with Mr. Lang?"

"We've had our differences," Jordan said. She set her project aside. "Surely you don't think I killed him?"

Jessica gave her a wide smile. "Don't worry, we're just trying to build a profile of his life right now."

"Right now," Jordan repeated.

"What can you tell us about Erik?" Peter asked quickly before Jordan could linger too long on that phrase.

Jordan linked her hands on her knees. "Erik and I both belong to a local environmentalist group. Right now, we are concerned about that new ski resort. The town hasn't given the company its permits yet and we've been fighting against it. The logging alone would decimate the local environment, not to mention the constant traffic from tourists. But as you can imagine, there are several... influential people in Pine Grove who only care about money, not the environment."

She spat out the words with so much venom that Peter's eyebrows rose. That seemed to be... well, more than what the situation called for.

Nolan dumped the contents of his dustpan into the garbage and nervously edged toward the back.

"Nolan, start mopping," Jordan ordered.

Nolan sighed and grabbed the mop bucket.

"You think there was a conspiracy?" Peter pressed.

"I wouldn't say conspiracy, exactly," Jordan sniffed. "But I will tell you this. There was no love lost between Captain Donnelly and Erik. It's not surprising that Donnelly wants to brush his murder under the rug. He's probably thinking 'good riddance' and all that."

"Why would you say that?" Jessica asked, frowning at Jordan.

Jordan squinted at her. "I understand why Myers would be here, but what business is it of yours? You're a vet. Aren't you too busy for this nonsense?"

"I'm helping Peter," Jessica answered with a sunny smile.

"That doesn't tell me why."

Jessica shrugged. "I was hoping to be able to find homes for a few of the animals at the shelter with the maze. Since it was shut down due to the body being found, I figure the sooner we get this over with, the sooner I can try again."

"Oh." Jordan nodded, accepting that explanation.

"So, you say that Lang and Donnelly didn't like each other?" Peter pressed, getting the conversation back on track.

Jordan turned her attention back to him. "They had quite a few run-ins. Donnelly arrested Erik more than once because Erik was fighting the good fight and Donnelly was in the pockets of corporations and politicians. I wouldn't be surprised if it was Donnelly himself who…" She trailed off, but the thought was obvious; Donnelly was on her suspect list.

The mop bucket slipped, spilling dirty water everywhere. Nolan winced and hurriedly started to try to clean it up. His shoulders were tight with tension as he worked.

Peter thought about it. While he didn't particularly like Donnelly himself, he didn't get 'corrupt cop' vibes off him. It was something to look closer into, though. If Donnelly had reason to kill Erik, he'd also want to cover it up.

That said, pretending like it was an accident seemed like a stupid way to do it. He might not have much hope for Donnelly's intelligence, but that seemed *too* stupid.

"Did you have any personal conflicts with Erik?" Peter pressed.

"We had our differences," Jordan said, sounding annoyed. "I already told you that. We disagreed on how to react to certain things, but our environmental goals were aligned. We wanted to stop that ski resort and protect the pristine forests around Pine Grove."

"Did you have your environmental meetings here?" Peter asked, deliberately not watching Nolan as he cleaned up the mess he'd just made. He was breathing heavily and there was sweat on his brow. Either he had a heart problem or he was very, very nervous about Peter and Jessica being around.

Jordan nodded. "You can join us if you want. We meet every Wednesday. Although right now we've adjourned meetings until Easter."

That long? Peter thanked Jordan for her time and turned away. His eye caught Nolan's and the younger man froze as though a searchlight had just been put on him. Peter felt Jordan's eyes on the back of his neck, so he left with Jessica. They wouldn't get anything while she was looming over their shoulder.

"I think Nolan knows something," Jessica murmured when they left the store.

Peter nodded. "I agree. We just have to find a way to speak with him alone."

CHAPTER FOUR

JESSICA FROWNED at the records from the environmental meetings that Jordan hosted. It seemed to her that this group was more about Jordan milking money out of people than it was about saving the environment. Maybe that was the basis of the 'disagreements' she had with Erik Lang. It was apparent that he didn't think they were doing enough, that they needed to offer the town alternatives.

The door to the clinic opened and she lifted her head, expecting an emergency—there were always emergencies just around the corner—but instead, it was Peter. Sam trotted faithfully beside him. His tail started to wag when he saw her.

"HOLD UP," Rina said, lifting both her hands. She cackled. "Dad, I didn't know that you wagged your tail."

Jessica laughed. She liked Rina's sense of humor. "No, I meant Sam's tail was wagging. You might think that he's super friendly, but those days he wasn't so confident. He was always looking up at Peter for reassurance, and it was only when Peter was relaxed that Sam ever wagged his tail."

Peter's eyes widened in surprise. "You noticed that?"

"I'm a vet. Of course, I noticed."

Matt and Rina exchanged devilish smiles. As Matt opened his mouth, though, Peter pointed at him. "No."

"Dad, if you're going to introduce us to your girlfriend, we have the right to tease you," Matt said, folding his arms.

Jessica shook her head. "They've got a point there."

Peter wrinkled his nose. "Let's just get back to the story."

"Woof," Sam said, sitting at Jessica's feet. He gave her an expectant look.

"It seems I've trained him into expecting tre—" Jessica started.

"Shhh!" Peter put a finger to his lips, his eyes sparkling. "Don't say it. It'll give him ideas. I'd like to get him off his 't-word' dependency."

He looked especially handsome like this, with his eyes sparkling and a clever grin on his lips. Jessica was unsurprised when her heart skipped a beat. She cleared her throat, hoping to clear her mind, and gestured for Peter to sit. "Did you find out anything from Donnelly?"

Peter had gotten a call from the captain shortly after leaving the Halloway Apothecary. Jessica hadn't heard anything they said, but it seemed that Peter had been hopeful when he left.

"The ME says it's murder," Peter answered. "Erik Lang was hit on the back of the head, but there's bruising on his shoulders that indicates he was held down in the water while he drowned."

Jessica shivered. "That's awful."

"It is, but at least it's a step in the right direction," Peter said. "What have you found out?"

"Erik told the environmental group that he uncovered several conspiracies and corruption in Pine Grove," Jessica answered. "He refused to talk about it, but suggested that there was at least one person in the group who was working for the corporations they fought against. It caused quite an upset. He said he was going to reveal the truth to the entire town as soon as he had the evidence."

"If there was a traitor in their midst, he certainly showed his hand by doing that," Peter said, his eyebrows furrowed. "I still think Nolan knows more than he wanted to let on. Did you have any luck in finding out more about him?"

Jessica nodded. "Nolan Grimm is the nephew of Howard Grimm, who owns a dairy farm. I regularly treat his animals. According to him, Nolan is a quiet kid who cares too much about what's going on in the world."

"What does that mean?"

"I'm not sure. Only that Howard thinks he's easily manipulated," Jessica said.

"Any idea of how we can talk with him?" Peter asked, looking thoughtful.

"He stays with his uncle. I thought we could drive out there tonight," Jessica said. "In the meantime, it looks like Erik was looking into several businesses and developers in town."

Peter rubbed his chin as he leaned in, peering at the documents Jessica pointed at. "And that means that our list of suspects has gotten even bigger. It could be anyone... We need to take a look at Erik's workshop. Maybe there will be clues there."

PETER DIDN'T LOOK FORWARD to talking with Donnelly again. The captain had been very sour when he admitted that he was wrong and it was a murder. He and Jessica weren't going to get into Erik Lang's place without police permission, though, so it was back to the station. Jessica went with him this time. As they went into the station, they found Donnelly putting on his jacket and hat.

"Captain," Jessica said, taking the lead—Donnelly had no reason to dislike her, and she assured Peter she could turn the charm on. "I have a favor to ask of you."

Donnelly tugged on his gloves. "What sort of favor, Dr. Stern? I'm a bit busy."

He eyed Peter with a suspicious look as Peter milled nearby. Peter tried to give him a non-threatening smile, but Donnelly only narrowed his eyes even further. Well, there went any hope that they'd start to get along. It was clear Donnelly had already made up his mind about what sort of person Peter was.

"We'd like to get into Erik Lang's studio and take a look around," Jessica said pleasantly, as though Donnelly wasn't glaring at Peter.

Donnelly's eyes snapped back at her. "Huh. Sure, why not? Not that it'll do much good. I already have my killer and I'm about to arrest him."

"Already?" Peter asked despite himself. "Well done, Captain. Who is it?"

Donnelly smiled and said the last name Peter could have expected. "Nolan Grimm. He's part of that little environmental group Erik was so fond of, but his uncle stands to get a huge profit for selling that farm of his for the ski resort. Nolan stands to inherit everything. It's obvious. He killed Erik so that he could inherit a few million, rather than some dirty farm."

CHAPTER
FIVE

DONNELLY REFUSED to let Jessica or Peter talk with Nolan. Though they'd planned to get right into the studio, Peter ended up spending several hours trying to get the information Donnelly had on Nolan, to see if there was a real case there. It wasn't until the Captain threatened to arrest him that Peter had to admit that he wasn't going to get anywhere.

So it wasn't until the next day that he and Jessica got to Erik Lang's studio. It was a large space divided up into several workstations. One of them was sketches of his sculptures, another was where he made the sculptures, and then a third space seemed to be for bookkeeping.

"Look at this," Jessica said as she looked through Erik's sketches. "It looks like he was dabbling in satire cartoons."

Peter leaned in closer to get a better look. As he did so, the scent of Jessica's shampoo wafted toward him. It caught him off-guard. It smelled clean and bright, unlike the heavily scented shampoos that you could find at most drugstores. Was that jasmine he was smelling?

"I think Jordan might have something," Jessia said, unaware of Peter's momentary lapse of concentration. "Take a look at this."

Peter shook himself. The page Jessica held out to him was a carica-ture of Captain Donnelly. His forehead and gut were both exaggerated as he sat on his haunches with an adoring look on his face. He wore a leash being held by a skier, presumably the person who wanted to open the ski resort. The skier waved a fan of money at Donnelly's face.

"Erik certainly had strong opinions," Jessica said, shaking her head. "And he really didn't like Donnelly."

"No, he didn't. It's funny, whenever I've heard about his artwork, his environmental activism never came up," Peter said. He looked through the other sketches. "But look at all this. He seemed to be really big on it. So why didn't that show in his work?"

Jessica gave him a puzzled look. "That is weird. It's obvious in all of his work."

"Is it?"

Jessica took his hand and pulled him over to where a half-finished sculpture sat. "Look at this. See how these waves here are falling, and how this part looks like the sun? The sculpture is about rising ocean levels, a global rise in temperature, and the changes in weather patterns that we're seeing. Summers are hotter, winters are colder, and we're experiencing more hurricanes than ever before."

Peter peered at the sculpture. Now that she pointed it out, it seemed obvious. He realized his hand was still in hers. The warmth felt nice, but he pulled away quickly. No matter how nice it was to hold her hand, or how good her hair smelled, or how pretty she was, it was too early for any of this. He hadn't been a divorced man for very long. The last thing he wanted to do was jump into a new relationship before he'd properly grown to know himself again.

"I love art," Jessica said, clasping her hands behind herself as she stared at the sculpture. There was a softness to her eyes and stance that made it very easy to forget everything he'd just said to himself.

Peter cleared his throat and turned away. "Wish there was more time to check out Lang's work, then. Unfortunately, that kid Donnelly arrested doesn't have much chance against the system if he's convicted."

"Right," Jessica murmured. Did she sound disappointed?

He nearly offered to take her to an art gallery up in the city, but managed to stop himself just in time. That was dangerous territory. He needed to keep his head in the game. He let out a shaky breath, unhappy at how he was reacting to all of this. He was going to have to put a lid on it if he planned to spend more time with Jessica.

"Hmm," he said as he came to a locked drawer. He tried it firmly but there was no budging it. "Have you seen a key anywhere?"

"No. Why?" Jessica walked over. "Oh, that's an interesting lock, isn't it? I wonder if the key is one of those old-fashioned ones."

"Could be," Peter said.

Both of them turned when they heard a soft scratching noise on the door to the studio. They exchanged alarmed looks. Peter wished he had brought his firearm along with him. It was locked in the safe back home. Despite not being convinced that Nolan Grimm was their killer, he hadn't thought there was any danger.

"Stand back," Peter told Jessica.

She ducked behind a desk, crouching out of sight.

Peter moved to the door and grabbed the handle. "Who's there?" he bellowed.

There was a pause on the other side, and then, "Woof!"

Wait! Was that... He flung the door open. Sam stepped into the studio, a doggy smile on his face.

"Sam! How did you find me?" Peter said, kneeling to pat his dog's head. "And how did you get out of the house? I thought I locked you in."

"Woof," Sam said.

Jessica emerged from her hiding spot and laughed. "We'll have to check for any loose windows when we take him back to your place. There was this one escape artist pooch I knew who would get into the attic of all places and get out through a hole in the chimney."

Peter scratched behind Sam's ears. "I don't want him to start running around town without me."

Sam started sniffing the area. He trotted into the studio. Peter and Jessica gave each other a mutually defeated look. It didn't seem like there was much here for them to investigate after all. Peter sighed.

"I suppose," he started.

"Woof!" Sam barked, scratching at something on the floor.

Peter went over to investigate. Sam pawed at the same spot. When Peter took a closer look, he saw a scrap of cloth pinned under the leg of the desk. It was part of a scarf... the same scarf that Leah had been wearing yesterday at the maze.

"It looks like we have a new suspect," Peter said, straightening. "Why do you think Leah Peabody would be here?"

CHAPTER
SIX

JESSICA RECEIVED a call that a dog was coming in lethargic and acting disoriented, so she rushed off to the vet clinic while Peter went to confront Leah. Sam seemed quite pleased with himself and kept begging for a treat. Every time he did so, Peter patted his head, scratched his ears, and told him he was a good boy. It was only when they got to Pine Grove's only grocery store that Peter realized that Sam might be training him.

Leah was on a break as Peter approached. She leaned against the side of the building, wrapped in a thick, oversized winter coat and a worn-out winter cap. She wore fingerless gloves as she took a long drag on her cigarette.

It always surprised Peter how different Leah had become. Back in high school, she was the star of the show everywhere she went. Now it seemed as though life had drained her to the point where she looked like nothing but a bitter, lonely woman. Peter knew he shouldn't judge —looks could be deceiving—but the sneer that crossed Leah's face when she caught sight of him certainly didn't help with the impression.

Still, he put on a polite expression as he came up to her. "Leah. Horrible business with Erik Lang, isn't it?"

She looked away from him. "Suppose so."

Peter waited a beat before he lifted the piece of her scarf. "Is this yours?"

"Hey, I've been looking for that." Leah snatched it from his hand. "This is my favorite scarf. I can still fix it."

Huh. The Leah he knew wouldn't be caught dead wearing last year's jeans. Either that scarf meant a lot to her, or she was having a really rough time of it right now.

"I found it in Erik Lang's studio," Peter said.

Leah's head jerked toward him. The cigarette dropped from her lips and lay smoldering on the sidewalk. "I wasn't anywhere near that snow maze!"

Peter frowned at her. "Two things about that. One, you were seen by multiple people." He'd confirmed with a handful of others at the booths that Leah had been hanging around. "Two, I didn't say anything about the maze. I was talking about Lang's studio."

"I didn't know him. There's no reason for my scarf to be there." She shoved the scrap into her pocket. "Maybe he stole it."

She stomped on her cigarette and glared at the black streak left behind on the snow.

Peter shook his head. "As far as lying goes, that's not very convincing, Leah."

She huffed and clawed her jacket tighter around herself. "Fine. Fine! We were… casually involved. We hung out sometimes. He was, um, practicing his oil painting and using me as a model. I went to the studio to, uh… collect the portraits. I didn't want them to be seen by everyone in town."

"I take it these portraits were of a… sensitive nature?" Peter probed carefully.

Leah's face went red. "Yes."

"I see." He ran a hand through his hair. "I'm going to have to confirm that, you understand. Will you be willing to show Jessica Stern?" he added quickly as Leah's expression grew alarmed. "I understand you not wanting to share them with me or Captain Donnelly."

Leah bit her lip, suddenly looking very vulnerable. She nodded. "I can do that. Although I think Donnelly knows already."

"Really?" Peter couldn't hide his shock.

"Yeah. He and Donnelly were always getting into these shouting matches, then would watch TV and drink beers. He came a few times while Erik was painting me. But he was a perfect gentleman about it," Leah added, sniffing. "Unlike *some* people."

Peter didn't see how he'd been ungentlemanly, but he was here for information. Pride didn't do well in these situations. "I'm sorry for making you uncomfortable, Leah. Can you tell me what they fought about?"

Leah shrugged. "As soon as Donnelly showed up, I left. I didn't want to get mixed up in that business. Erik told me once that he was a spy working with the police, though," she added. "And that he was going to blow the lid off the corruption of that anti-ski group. I don't know why they're so against it. It's too expensive to go to Vermont to ski, having something right close to Pine Grove will mean that us locals can ski once in a while."

She fished in her pocket for a fresh cigarette, which she lit. Peter moved slightly to be upwind of the smoke as it billowed around her.

"Do you recall ever seeing Nolan Grimm at Erik's place?" Peter asked.

"Yeah, once. He was sneaking around when I left." Leah shrugged. "But it looked to me like Erik was expecting him. If you ask me," she took another drag on her cigarette, "Donnelly arrested the wrong man. Nolan Grimm is a weakling. He wouldn't have the guts to kill Erik."

NOLAN LIVED on his uncle's dairy farm, but not in the same house. There was a small, studio cottage near the edge of the property, far away from the milking barns, where Nolan called home. It was painfully neat and organized. Peter had seen hotel rooms that were less put together than Nolan's space. Everything was organic and environmentally friendly.

"I think this is handmade," Jessica said as she leaned over a loom in one corner. "And he's weaving his own cloth. Look at this." She picked up a notebook. "He's been harvesting invasive plants from the forest and using them to make cloth and baskets."

"Wow. That's dedication," Peter said, admiring the kid. He went to a window and frowned. "Which begs the question why he has a burn barrel right next to the house."

Jessica joined him. "He seems more like the type that would recycle everything he could rather than burn it."

"My thoughts exactly."

They went outside and inspected the burn barrel. Inside was a hunk of melted plastic clinging to remnants of a fire. Something shiny lay in the midst of it. Peter pulled on a latex glove and reached in to pull it out. It was a metal rod about twelve inches long.

"Looks like an ice pick," Jessica said. "And that plastic could be part of the handle."

"There's something written here," Peter said, squinting. He turned the rod to catch the light better and the etching became clear. He let out a heavy sigh as he read aloud. "First Prize, Erik Lang."

CHAPTER
SEVEN

JESSICA RAN a hand over her eyes. "I think I know what this is. Last year, Erik competed in a national ice sculpting competition. The first prize was a trophy shaped like an ice pick. Nolan had to have taken this from Erik's studio. Do you think he killed Erik with it?"

Peter put the pick in an evidence bag. "No. Donnelly said that Erik was hit over the head, and then held under the water until he drowned. That doesn't line up with this trophy. Judging from the amount of plastic left over, it wouldn't have been heavy enough. But Nolan did take it. It's funny that Donnelly is convinced that Nolan killed Erik, but didn't find this."

"True, but maybe he knows something we don't," Jessica suggested.

That was a possibility, yes. So far, Peter's impression of the man left a lot to be desired. Maybe Donnelly had more up his sleeve than Peter gave him credit for.

"Nolan was very nervous that day we spoke with Jordan," he said slowly. "Maybe he was playing the double agent, so to say. He might have been the 'corruption' Erik said was in the environmental group. He might have been sent in there to cause disruption so they wouldn't organize enough to stop the ski resort."

Jessica nodded as she ran her hands through her long hair. "I get what you're saying, but look at everything in his home. This is a lot to do if he didn't actually believe in what he was doing."

Peter agreed. He rubbed his chin as he viewed the house. "The case does seem pretty sloppy. If he's guilty, why would he act so suspiciously in public rather than lying low?"

"That's a good point." Jessica hesitated. "I don't want to believe that Nolan was involved in the murder. Do you think that we're letting our personal opinions affect our judgment too much? I can't think of anyone it might have been if it wasn't Nolan."

"And that's where the killer wants us to be. If Nolan is the only suspect, then the real killer gets off free," Peter said, nodding to himself. It all made sense now. "Someone else is the corruption. They decided Nolan was an easy target since he was already seen hanging around Erik. No doubt they're afraid he'll pick up where Erik left off, too, and so decided to get rid of him. Two birds, one stone."

Jessica frowned. "So, our killer is setting up that sweet kid."

"I think so." Peter snapped a picture of the barrel. "I think it's time we went to talk with Captain Donnelly and got all the facts."

They walked back to the car. Jessica watched Peter intently, as though she was trying to read his mind. The intense focus was slightly unnerving if he was honest. He wasn't used to people paying that close attention to him. One of the things he'd always taken pride in was his everyman appearance. It allowed him to get close to suspects and gain their trust more easily.

"Do you think Donnelly is the killer?" she asked once they were in the car.

Peter's hands tightened on the wheel. "I don't know. But if he is, he has to face justice."

DONNELLY SQUINTED SUSPICIOUSLY AT PETER, ignoring Jessica entirely. She thought the man was the kind that automatically disliked everyone until they gave him a reason to stop. Then he was ambivalent toward them. If what Leah told Peter was true, that he and Erik used to fight and drink beers together, he might have lost his best friend.

"I don't think you need to know anything about my case," Donnelly said. "I'm not going to hand over all my evidence to the likes of you."

"You found Nolan's prints at the scene, right?" Jessica asked.

Donnelly and Peter both gave her surprised looks. She understood Donnelly's surprise—"How did you know that?" he blustered—but Peter was another story. She couldn't get a full read on the man. He was smart and genial, but there was a razor mind behind that handsome face. He played it close to the vest... and she wanted to learn more about him.

"We heard from Leah Peabody that Nolan sometimes would spend time at Erik's studio," Jessica said. "So, it makes sense his prints were there."

"Captain, perhaps I can make a call to my FBI contacts," Peter suggested. "It might be helpful."

Donnelly puffed up his chest. "Is that a threat, Myers?"

Peter shook his head, though it had sounded vaguely like a threat. "An offer, Captain."

Donnelly kept squinting at him from one way to the other, as though he expected Peter to suddenly pull a gun from his hip. Finally, he grunted and leaned back at his desk. "The corporation that wants to put in the ski resort has been having a lot of issues with Halloway's environmental group. They kept hounding me, so I was paying special attention to make sure they didn't do anything crazy."

Jessica shared a look with Peter. "I don't wish to be indelicate," she said slowly, "but we found a rather... unflattering cartoon of you at Erik's studio, implying that you were being paid off by the ski resort."

"I saw that thing," Donnelly said, and to Jessica's surprise, he laughed. "It was our idea. I'm not in anyone's pocket. Erik told me that the resort was breaking several laws. I believed him. We were trying to figure out what was happening, and we figured if people thought I was complicit, they'd trust me with evidence more."

Peter's eyebrows lifted toward his hairline. "That's clever."

Donnelly glared at him. "Try to look more surprised. Erik was working on finding me an environmental report that implicated the resort in illegal logging. He was sure someone in his group was leaking information. Before he died, he told me he thought it was Nolan."

"So that's why you arrested him," Jessica murmured.

"That's right." Donnelly laced his fingers over his thick waist. "I think Erik found evidence. And Nolan killed him for it."

CHAPTER
EIGHT

PETER WAS ashamed to admit how surprised he was. He'd assumed Donnelly was a shifty, bumbling man who cared more about himself than anyone else. It seemed like he had a few things to learn about Pine Grove. He might have grown up here, but his time in the big city had left him jaded. He didn't know this place as well as he thought he did.

And that was a good thing. It meant he had more to learn, which in turn meant he wasn't going to grow stale living in this place.

"Captain, I know you don't trust me because of my family history," Peter said. "But if you'll look at my record with the FBI, you'll see that I put away a lot of bad people."

"I checked you out," Donnelly said, seeming reluctant. "Big shot FBI lawyer. I don't trust lawyers, you know. But it seems like you might be halfway decent."

Peter bit back on a retort. He was one of the leading lawyers in the Bureau for a reason. This was as close to a compliment that Donnelly had given him, though, so he only nodded once and kept quiet. Sometimes the best way to convince a person was to not talk at all.

"Fine," Donnelly grunted. "You can talk with Nolan. Half an hour."

Peter nodded his thanks. He and Jessica followed Donnelly into the holding cells. Nolan sat on a long, hard bench, his head in his hands.

When he looked up, his eyes were red from crying. Peter thought about what they'd found at his place, and how intense he seemed about all this environmental stuff. He was clearly a soft-hearted kid. Peter felt a twinge of sympathy for him.

"Hello, Nolan," Peter said as he came into the cell. "We'd like to talk to you about what happened that night with Erik."

Nolan wiped his eyes on his sleeve. "Do you think I killed him, too?"

"No," Jessica said gently as she sat next to him. "But we know you were there. What happened?"

Nolan fidgeted with his sleeve as he answered. "Erik asked me to poke around the group. He was convinced someone was leaking information to the ski resort. I thought he was full of it. That night, I went to talk to him about it. I tried to get him to tell me why he was so convinced there was someone leaking information. He refused to tell me anything.

"I made the mistake of getting upset. I told him he was making it all up because he wanted to make more of a name for his art. I told him he was fake because of the water usage in his artwork. He got angry at me. Started to yell and he kept coming at me like he was going to attack." Nolan shuddered. "I panicked. There was an ice pick trophy sitting on the shelf and I grabbed it to defend myself. But I didn't kill him! He told me to leave so I did. I went home. And the next morning I heard he'd been killed by an ice pick. I panicked again, thinking someone would find the one I took and think I killed him. So, I burned it."

Peter nodded slowly. That fit with the evidence that they'd collected. "We could have done tests on the pick, to see if there was blood on it."

"I didn't think about that," Nolan mumbled. "Now I have no way to prove I didn't do it."

"You might not." Jessica pulled out her phone. "But we have something. For one thing, Erik wasn't killed by an ice pick. For another…" She opened her phone and flipped through the photos. Peter leaned forward as she stopped on a cartoon that displayed an obvious take on

Nolan. He held an ice pick and looked bewildered under the caption, *Everyone's a tool for hire.*

"He must have drawn that after your argument," Peter said.

Nolan frowned. "You mean you believe me?"

"Erik had to have time to draw that after your fight and before he died. He thought you were the leak," Peter added.

"Me?" Nolan yelped. "Why would he suspect me?"

That was a very good question. Why indeed? They needed to get back to his studio and get into that locked drawer. Peter had a feeling that it contained the information they needed to bust this case wide open.

Donnelly begrudgingly accompanied them to the studio and got a locksmith to open up the drawer. Inside were various financial records that indeed linked Nolan to the resort's payroll. It quickly became apparent, though, that it wasn't quite… normal. Jessica, being used to paying employees at the vet clinic, soon pointed out some very strange coincidences.

The payment periods matched precisely those Nolan expected from working at Halloway's Apothecary, and coincidentally lined up perfectly with the hours he worked at the place.

"They're directly depositing into Nolan's bank account as though he's being paid by the Apothecary," Peter said, understanding what this meant. "So that must mean the resort is paying off Jordan Halloway, but framing it as Nolan being paid off. And Nolan thinks these are just his wages."

"I'll bet if we look into the Apothecary records, it lists Nolan as a volunteer," Jessica said.

Donnelly frowned at the records. "So, Jordan Halloway was the leak."

Jessica laid a hand on his arm. "I have an idea of how to prove this all. But we're going to need your help, Richard… and you're going to have to trust Peter to wear a wire."

CHAPTER
NINE

IT WAS LATE, after the Apothecary's hours, when Peter stepped through the doors. That same strange scent that had bothered him before wafted over him again. It made his eyes water and he bit back a cough. He couldn't help but think that Jordan's whole shtick here was fake. She was selling out the local environment to the ski resort. How much of this was real, and how much was just because she thought it was a market to tap into?

"Oh, it's you." Jordan held a broom awkwardly in her hands. "We're closed."

Peter smiled. "Oh, that's alright. I'm here looking for… you could call it a job. Since your worker was sent to jail for a murder you framed him for."

Jordan's eyes widened. "I beg your pardon?"

"I know it all, Jordan. You've been paid off by the ski resort. You had them funnel the money directly into Nolan's account so you could write him off as a volunteer. Not only did you get his labor for free, but you also got a nice little tax break, didn't you?" Peter's smile widened. "But you didn't hide your trail very well. Erik Lang figured it out as easily as I did. And when he confronted you, you killed him."

"I don't know what you're talking about," Jordan said, narrowing her eyes. "Now if you'll excuse me—"

"You weren't alone that night," Peter interrupted, taking a gamble. Jordan fell silent.

"Erik knew I used to work for the FBI and he contacted me. You see, he thought Donnelly was in on it—turns out, he's just incompetent." Peter paused, hoping that Donnelly—listening from outside—didn't take that too personally. He laughed and continued. "You look pale, Jordan. Not as pale as Erik did after you drowned him."

"What do you want?" Jordan demanded as she went to the cash register.

Peter shrugged. "Simple. I want a cut. Half sounds fair, doesn't it? To keep your secret?"'

Jordan whipped a pistol out from behind the desk. "Oh, I'll tell you what sounds fair," she snarled. "You showed your hand, Myers! You don't have any proof I killed Erik, just you as a witness. Well, you know what they say. Dead men tell no—"

The door flew open. Jordan's gun went off and Peter dove to the side. The bullet whistled through the air, narrowly missing him. He landed hard on the floor as Jordan dropped the gun and threw her hands into the air. Within minutes, it was over.

Back at the station, Donnelly traded Nolan out in the cell for Jordan. He glared at Peter, but it seemed more out of principle than anything else.

"Well. Seems like you got her to confess," Donnelly said, folding his arms. "And this gives me evidence to go against the ski resort. It just might end up that Erik Lang stopped the blasted thing by getting himself murdered. The idiot."

Ah, so they were friends. Donnelly's mouth pulled into a tighter line as he spoke and his voice shook ever so slightly.

"It's a good thing he's got you to carry on his work," Peter said. He made to put a bracing hand on Donnelly's shoulder, but Donnelly stepped away and glared at him as though Peter had pulled a gun on him. Peter awkwardly turned the gesture into a thumbs-up instead.

"Those papers we found in Erik's drawer will be of use," Jessica added, stepping in to fill the awkward silence. "You've got leads to follow when taking down that ski resort. I wouldn't be surprised if their corruption runs even deeper than we realize."

Donnelly nodded. "Yeah. Like they have mob ties."

Another glare in Peter's direction. Peter let it roll off his back. He had time to prove that he wasn't like his father to Donnelly. Though, with any luck, he wouldn't have much business that brought him close to the captain again.

He and Jessica took their leave. Peter yawned as they left the police station. He hadn't been sleeping much, too busy trying to figure out this case. Jessica gave him a concerned look and held out her hand.

"Give me your keys."

"That's not necessary," Peter said in surprise.

"I'll be the judge of that. Besides, we still need to figure out how Sam broke out of your house. Now hand them over." She gave him a stern look, then mimicked the distrustful glare Donnelly had given him. Peter laughed and relented.

As it turned out, they got back to his place just at the right time. Sam was in the process of wiggling out of a window in the basement. Peter could have sworn that he'd locked it, but when he checked, he found the lock was broken. He shook his head in amazement as Sam leaned up against him, wagging his tail happily.

"Either you're one strong dog or that was one weak lock," Peter said.

"Woof," Sam replied. Was it just Peter's imagination that he sounded boastful?

Peter straightened and turned to Jessica, who stood nearby with her hands tucked into her pockets. "Now that mystery is solved, do you want to come in for a cup of coffee?"

"Coffee? This late?" Jessica shook her head. "No wonder you're yawning so much. You must stay up all night!"

Peter laughed. "Hot chocolate, then."

Jessica grinned. "Sounds great. You know, I really enjoyed working with you to solve this murder. We should do it again. If there are any more murders in Pine Grove, that is," she added, grimacing. "And I hope there aren't."

"If there are, I know where to come," Peter quipped.

As he let her into the house, he caught the scent of her shampoo again. He considered making up an excuse to rescind the offer of hot chocolate, but stopped himself. He needed friends here in Pine Grove. Maybe Jessica was the friend he needed.

As for these other feelings… well, he'd deal with them in due time. He'd come to Pine Grove for a fresh start. And he might have found one.

EPILOGUE

"SO DOES DONNELLY LIKE YOU NOW?" Matt asked, quirking an eyebrow at Peter. "Since you helped him so much over the past five years?"

Peter and Jessica shared an ironic look. "No. Donnelly still dislikes me as much as ever. I get the sense he's just waiting for me to turn to the dark side or some such thing. That, or he thinks that when I solve the cases around town, I'm thumbing my nose at him."

"Too bad," Rina said. She eyed the chocolate swirl left on her dessert plate as though she was debating whether to lick it clean. Despite everything he and Melanie tried with their daughter, Rina had never let a little thing like good manners stop her from enjoying every last morsel of a meal.

"If you lick your plate, I'm not inviting you to the wedding," Matt threatened.

It apparently was effective, because Rina folded her arms and leaned back with a huff. "Fine, fine. But I don't know why they leave so much deliciousness on the plate if they're not going to make it socially acceptable to get every single last piece."

Peter pushed back his chair. Sam lifted his head and wagged his tail once. "Well, this was a great meal. I'll go pay and we can head out."

"I've got to call it a night, unfortunately," Jessica said. "Early morning."

Peter paid, said his goodbyes to Jessica, then headed back to his place with Rina and Matt. Rina smothered Sam with attention as they drove and he drank it all up. Once they were back at Peter's place, his kids threw themselves onto the sofa and grinned at him.

"I like her," Rina declared. "She's got this great elegant sort of aura around her. She's cool."

Matt nodded his agreement. "I like her, too. I'm just curious… how serious is it between you two?"

Peter took a seat in the overstuffed chair near the fireplace. "We're moving at a comfortable pace. We're not in a rush for anything super serious, but we're not holding ourselves back, either. Does that answer you?"

"I think so," Matt said. He grinned at his father. "I'm not sure if it's Jessica or Pine Grove, but you're looking great, Dad."

Rina pointed at him. "That's it exactly. You seem happy here. Happier than you were… before."

Peter smiled gratefully at them. "I am happy here. That's not to say I wasn't happy before," he added. "I wouldn't trade the years with your mom and you two for anything. I just think it's natural that as people get older, they become more comfortable with themselves and can figure out what truly makes them happy, rather than chasing after what they think makes them happy."

"I hope so," Rina said.

Peter smiled at her. "You'll get there. You both will. One day you'll have your own Pine Grove."

Rina's eyes went wide. "Oooh, I hope not! I don't want a whole town—too much responsibility!"

And then she burst out into laughter at her own joke. Peter chuckled, amused at her amusement. His kids liking Jessica was a huge weight off his shoulders. He was happy here. And he was glad they were happy for him.

The End

LUCK RUNS OUT

A COZY MYSTERY

PROLOGUE

ST. Patrick's Day was always a busy day for Connor O'Hara. Owning an Irish Pub in a town as small as Pine Grove had that effect. Normally, he enjoyed the atmosphere. The drinking, the singing, the shamrocks everywhere you turned. It was a way for him to connect to his ancestral roots and earn a handsome amount of cash at the same time.

Today, though, a dark cloud hung over his head as he strung up green garlands. He was late on decorating. Normally, he'd have had this place decked out days ago. It looked like he was going to miss the St. Paddy's Parade. Just his luck. The parade had been his favorite part of the holiday since he and his brother were put in the back of their dad's old pickup and threw handfuls of candy at the crowd.

"Cheer up, Connor," he told himself. "It's not like this is the last year you'll be able to see the parade."

"Needs to be a bit higher," a high, sweet voice said behind him.

Connor turned, his mood instantly lightening. Maeve Anderson, his bartender, had that effect on him. She grinned at him behind a pair of green, cat-eye glasses. She wore a truly massive red wig with curls that rivaled the fluffiness of a cloud.

"Lookin' good," he told her as he descended from the ladder. "Lookin' real Irish there, girl."

Maeve put one hand under her chin and struck a pose. "I do have some Irish in me. My great-great-great-grandmother was Irish. That's why red looks good on me. Maybe I should dye my hair. What do you think?"

Connor caught a strand of loose hair that hadn't gotten tucked in under the wig. Her dark brown hair was starting to streak with silver. "I dunno. I think you've got a natural charm that'd only be hidden by dyes and whatnot. Though you'd still be a fox if you shaved your head bald."

"Charmer," Maeve said, swatting his chest playfully. "You keep that up and I'm going to start demanding you buy me a drink. Now. What's got you in such a grumpy mood today of all days?"

Connor sighed. "It's personal stuff. I'm having some trouble with Liam."

Maeve fought not to scowl at hearing the name of Connor's estranged younger brother. "He's sniffing around again?"

"Yeah. But that's not the worst of it. I've been getting some… disturbing notes," he admitted. He didn't want to go into full detail with Maeve, didn't want to worry her. It was probably just his dumb brother trying to frighten him.

"How disturbing?" Maeve demanded.

Connor grinned at her, refusing to put his burden on her shoulders. "Oh, you know. Love letters and the like."

Maeve folded her arms. "Connor O'Hara, we've known each other for over twenty years. Something clearly has you worried. Has Liam gotten himself involved in something? Are you worried about him?"

"No. Not at all. You know I decided long ago I couldn't waste any more time on him," Connor said, not meeting her eye.

Maeve cupped his cheek and turned him toward her. "Then what's going on? You can tell me."

Connor hesitated. The threatening letters had been getting worse of late. He'd even considered going to Captain Richard Donnelly, but what could he do about it? Connor remembered all too well when his father had gone missing. Donnelly just said 'There's nothing I can do' after two days of searching.

The worst thing about it was that Connor never knew what happened to his old man. One day he was going up to the lake to go fishing… and that was the last anyone had seen him. It'd destroyed his mother. She didn't hold out long after they lost his father. Between the stress of the pub, grief, and the troubles Liam kept bringing to their door… she just couldn't take it.

"There's nothing to be worried about," Connor said, forcing himself to speak with more confidence than he felt. He gave Maeve a grin. No use in worrying her more than he'd already done. "I'll deal with it. And as far as Liam goes, Fio's back in town for a few days. She'll know how to deal with him."

Maeve nodded. "If you need anything, you let me know."

"Of course," Connor said. He smiled at her cloud-like wig as she moved behind the bar. One of these days, he might just have to ask that woman to marry him.

CHAPTER
ONE

PETER MYER, former FBI lawyer and current amateur artist, stood next to Dr. Jessica Stern, veterinarian extraordinaire, and cheered as a large float covered in shamrocks and beer kegs passed by. Several people dressed up as leprechauns raced around the float, passing out non-alcoholic beers to the crowd. It was a spectacular display. He eagerly craned his neck to watch the float as it passed.

"See?" Jessica laughed. "I told you you'd like the St. Patrick's parade."

"Yeah, you were right," Peter agreed.

Normally he wasn't much into parades, but after a hard winter, this was a welcome distraction. His fingers itched to try to paint the scene he saw. Since he'd taken up painting, he that everything ended up being something he wanted to transform into acrylics on canvas.

Peter slid his hand into Jessica's, smiling at her as he distractedly watched for the next float. "You were right about leaving Sam at home, too. This would have overexcited him."

Winter still clung on here and there with patches of snow having turned a dirty brown. It would have been depressing if it weren't for the promise of spring just around the corner. The sheer amount of vibrant green that the town was bathed in for the holiday was enough of a promise of what was to come that it lifted everyone's spirits.

Life had grown quiet in Pine Grove again. The last case Peter found himself involved in had been the murder of a local artist by the name of Alan, but that was nearly two years ago now. Last summer, Peter had introduced Jessica to his grown kids, Rina and Matt. This year, his ex-wife Melanie had called to offer him use of her cabin on the lake if he wanted a summer trip with the kids. She'd been quick to say Jessica was welcome to go with them if he wanted.

Peter suspected Melanie was getting married soon. He'd find out in April, when Matt was getting married. He was looking forward to the wedding, as was Jessica; she'd been touched and thrilled to receive an invite to attend.

He squeezed Jessica's hand a little tighter when a piercing scream broke through the festive atmosphere. He turned to see Maeve, the bartender at O'Hara's, stumbling out of the pub. She wore a red wig styled like an 80s rock star.

"Help me," she called. "It's Connor! I think he's dead."

Peter hurried forward, Jessica hot on his heels. Maeve clutched her chest, her blue eyes wide behind a pair of lopsided glasses.

"Where is he?" Peter asked gently.

"The basement," Maeve answered.

Jessica put an arm around Maeve and carefully led her into the pub, away from the prying eyes of the crowd. Peter scanned and nodded to himself when he saw Donnelly making his way to the pub. Good. They needed the police to be part of this. He waited for the police captain to join him before heading down into the basement.

Connor O'Hara was definitely dead.

"Poor chap broke his neck," Captain Donnelly said, shaking his head. "I've already called the ambulance. Better call the morgue, too."

Peter studied the scene before him. Connor's body lay at a strange angle, one that clearly showed he had broken his neck in the fall. Spilled beer splashed all around the basement, as though he'd been drinking when he fell. The ladder, an old wooden thing, lay broken at his feet.

"Looks like he'd decided to have a drink while he fixed that light-bulb," Donnelly said, pointing at the empty socket above them. The light came from outside. Connor had rigged up a mirror system to reflect the sunlight around the basement, presumably to save on electricity on sunny days. "The ladder broke and he lost his balance. He fell and…"

Donnelly shook his head sadly.

It was hard to take him seriously when the green antennae ending with gold stars he wore on his head bounced around like that. Peter was distracted by the movement, staring openly. He didn't mean to. After all, Donnelly didn't like him on the best of days. He was just surprised to see the normally glaring and scowling police captain looking so… festive.

Donnelly caught him staring and snatched the headband off. "My Da was from Ireland."

Peter nodded once. "Did you notice the bruises on Connor's wrists?"

"Bruises?" Donnelly crouched near the body. He scratched his head. "Huh. Looks like…" He held his own arms out and then turned them as though he was fending off an attack. "Defensive injuries. And there's a whiskey bottle under the shelf here. Looks like it's got blood on it."

"Is it broken?" Peter asked

Donnelly straightened. "Doesn't look like it. These bottles are surprisingly strong, you know. It takes quite a bit of force to break them. It's not like in the movies."

"Looks like he has something in his pocket," Peter said, pointing at a lump on Connor's chest.

"Right." Donnelly held out a hand, stopping Peter as he started to bend. "No touching anything until forensics arrives. It might look like an accident at first glance, but this has got all the makings of a murder."

Peter nodded slowly. He had come to the same conclusion. Donnelly put his hands on his hips as he glared down at Connor's body. It was a rather hostile look to give an already dead man. Had the police captain had trouble with Connor?

"I didn't know him well," Peter said, fishing for information. "I liked him, though. He always welcomed dogs into the pub and was always great with Sam."

Donnelly lifted his head. "Yeah, he was crazy for animals. One of his more obvious flaws. But he didn't cause me trouble, unlike that no-good brother of his."

"You seemed pretty deep in thought," Peter said. "If Connor didn't give you trouble, then what's it about?"

"Just remembering his old man's case."

Peter's eyes widened. "His father was murdered?"

"Probably. About ten years ago now, his father went up to the lake to do some fishing. Disappeared. I always thought he must have seen something he shouldn't have. Got himself caught in some mob hit or something." Donnelly folded his arms as he gave Peter a shrewd look. "Speaking of which, how's Marconi?"

Donnelly never liked the Myers. He'd known about Peter's father having ties to the mob. Peter himself, a lawyer like his dad, hadn't known about the connections until after he'd moved back to Pine Grove after his divorce.

Marconi, a mob thug who sometimes stopped in Pine Grove, had developed ties to Peter that Peter didn't like. Marconi had given him the clues he'd needed to solve a case or two over the years. He knew there was more to it than Marconi was letting on, but he hadn't been able to figure it out.

Did Donnelly think the mob was behind Connor's death?

"I haven't talked to Marconi in over a year," Peter answered quietly. "But the next time I see him, I'll let you know."

"Good," Donnelly said. He turned back to the body and resumed his glaring.

CHAPTER
TWO

JESSICA RUBBED Maeve's arm as the older woman sniffled into a handkerchief. She'd discarded her wig and funky glasses. The transformation was impressive. Without her getup, she looked much more delicate. Jessica couldn't remember a time when Maeve didn't work at the O'Hara pub. She must be very close to the family.

"I knew something was wrong," Maeve murmured into her handkerchief. "I knew it. He was acting so strangely…"

"Strangely?" Jessica prompted.

Maeve hesitated, as though she was worried about betraying a confidence. "He was getting paranoid. Double-checking the locks. Wouldn't let me stay late by myself or open without him. I asked him about it and he tried to play it off as though he wanted to spend more time with me, but there were a few times when the dog started barking and he got nervous."

"You have a dog here at the pub?" Jessica asked in surprise.

"He's Connor's dog. Lives upstairs with him," Maeve said. "His name is Pogo and he's a bit of a… well, he's a good dog, but he doesn't get along with people all too well."

"So, he's aggressive?" Jessica prodded. She owned the only veterinary clinic here in Pine Grove. Was Pogo's aggression the reason Connor had never brought him in? Maybe he had a vet in the city?

Maeve sighed. "He can be, yeah. Connor always took him for long walks in the morning, before the town woke up so they wouldn't run into anyone else."

"Where was Pogo when Connor died?" Jessica asked her, following a hunch.

"He was upstairs, like usual. He's been acting a bit unusual lately, too. I thought he was picking up Connor's stress but he seems... shyer than normal, I suppose? Maybe you can take a look at him?" Maeve suggested. "I'll have to put a muzzle on him, though. He doesn't like vets very much."

Jessica nodded her understanding. She'd been bitten enough times to know even the sweetest dog would defend itself when it was in pain. She also knew that aggression was often spurred by fear. She wondered what sort of aggressive dog Pogo was. She waited downstairs while Maeve went for Pogo.

While she was gone, Peter came up from the basement. From the look on his face, Jessica knew. It was another murder in Pine Grove.

"Maeve is getting Connor's dog for me to look at," she told him under her breath. She explained what she learned quickly and he did the same. Once they were done, Peter slipped his hand into hers and squeezed lightly. Jessica was grateful for the comfort. She enjoyed investigating mysteries with Peter, but usually, the people who died weren't ones she knew well.

She wouldn't say she was friends with Connor O'Hara, but she did know him. It hurt differently.

Maeve returned shortly, coaxing a large rottweiler with her. The big dog pressed up against her legs, whining and whimpering. He started to shake like a leaf when he saw Peter and then stiffened, growling at Jessica.

"Whoa," Peter said, instantly moving to stand in front of Jessica.

"Peter, it's okay." Jessica put a hand on his arm. "He's muzzled. Hey, sweet boy," she said in a low, soothing voice to the dog. "Can I come closer?"

She stepped forward. Pogo jerked against the thick leash Maeve held and growled again.

"He's frightened," Jessica observed. "Less mean and more reacting out of fear. It's okay, Pogo. I won't come any closer. Can you get him to sit?" she asked Maeve. "I think I see something on his stomach."

It took some coaxing, but Maeve did get Pogo to sit. He panted, his ribs heaving, and he kept looking up at Maeve and licking his lips. Clearly, he wanted her to take him out of this situation. Jessica's lips pressed together as she peered at him from where she was.

"He's got bruises on his stomach," she said. "Do you know if Connor took him to a vet at all recently?"

Maeve's eyes were wide. "I think he took him up to the city recently. Bruises! What happened to you, boy?"

"Maybe he had a bad encounter with someone out on a walk," Jessica suggested, anger boiling in her chest. "It looks to me like he was kicked."

Maeve dropped to her knees and gently cradled Pogo's massive head in her hands. "Oh, you poor boy. Who would kick you?" She rubbed his ears lightly and some of the tension in Pogo's body eased off.

Peter cleared his throat. "I hate to ask this, but could Connor have been abusing his dog?"

"Never!" Maeve looked up, her watery gaze confident. "He would never lay a hand on anyone. Connor was the sweetest guy. Just ask anyone who came to the bar. Even when customers got out of hand, he never hurt anyone. He took more than one punch in his day, but I've never seen him lose his temper, not even with his brother."

PETER MADE note of the way Maeve talked about Connor's brother. There was clearly bad blood there. He rubbed his chin as he considered the facts as he knew them. Connor had been acting paranoid lately, coinciding with when his dog started to act strangely, too. The two could be connected. It was likely to have something to do with his brother.

"Can you tell us anything about Liam O'Hara?" Peter asked Maeve.

"Nothing good," Maeve answered with more vitriol than Peter expected. She winced and hugged Pogo a little closer. "I'm sorry, but I don't know why you're asking. Unless you think he kicked Pogo?"

Peter took a deep breath. "I'm sorry, but it looks like Connor was murdered."

Maeve gasped. "Murdered!"

"Can you think of anyone who might want to hurt him?" Peter asked.

"No! He and Liam didn't get along and Liam is... well, he isn't exactly what I'd call an upstanding citizen, but he's not a violent man." Maeve clutched at her chest. "Murdered. I can't think of anyone who would want to hurt that gentle soul."

The door to the back rooms opened. A tall, black-haired woman dressed in a slinky green dress walked in. She smiled charmingly at Peter and Jessica, but it dropped when Pogo stiffened and growled.

"What's that dog doing down here?" she asked, nervously sliding behind the bar. "Maeve, you know he doesn't like people."

Maeve straightened. "This is Fiona O'Hara, Connor's cousin. Fio... Connor is dead. This is Peter and Jessica. They're working with the police. They think it was a murder."

Fiona's face went ashen. She clutched at the bar, opening and closing her mouth several times. "Dead? Oh, Maeve. I'm so sorry. I—" She started forward but stopped and looked at Pogo warily. "Oh, I guess this means Liam will inherit..." She sucked in a deep breath and shook her head. "Why don't you take Pogo back upstairs, Maeve? He'll get nervous with people coming in and out."

Peter made a mental note. So, Liam stood to inherit the pub. Despite what Maeve said about not believing he'd hurt anyone... well, that was the motive. The oldest in the book.

CHAPTER
THREE

LATER THAT DAY, Donnelly told Peter to stop by the station. Peter in turn asked Jessica to accompany him. Donnelly was always more polite in the presence of a lady. They arrived shortly before dinner time. Donnelly was at his desk, typing furiously at his computer. His meaty hands, which Peter thought looked more suited to hard labor like chopping wood than working electronics, slammed against the keyboard with such force it was like he was trying to break it.

Donnelly looked up and gave Peter his characteristic suspicious look. "Myer. Dr. Stern. Got this off Connor's body." He grabbed a small, linen-bound notebook. "Seems like he kept a journal. Maybe it'll help your investigation."

"Our investigation?" Jessica asked, her eyebrows quirked. "You're just handing it over to us?"

"Why not?" Donnelly's scowl deepened.

Peter stepped forward for the journal, his mind racing over Donnelly's sudden change of attitude.

"Even if I try to stop you, you'll just keep poking around. For once you'll be working with me instead of trying to make a fool out of me," Donnelly continued.

Ah, there it was. "Captain, it's never been my intention to make a fool out of you."

"Sure coulda fooled... the town," Donnelly grunted. "Besides, I already took a read through it. There's nothing in there I didn't already know."

"Is there anything new about the cause of death?" Peter asked.

Donnelly's frown deepened and he rolled his eyes. "It's only been a few hours, Myer. The ME hasn't finished going over the body yet. Were you this impatient when working with the FBI?"

"I didn't investigate murders with the FBI. Only prosecuted the killers," Peter replied.

"Maybe you should go back to it," Donnelly muttered as he turned back to his computer.

Peter and Jessica left the station and headed to their favorite café. As they waited for their food, they skimmed through the journal, their shoulders brushing against each other. They'd already heard about the dispute between Connor and his brother, but the depth of it soon became clear. Liam had been cut out from their parents' will entirely, and he'd been fighting Connor ever since their father's death.

"Looks like it wasn't just the pub," Peter said, pointing out a passage in the journal. "The O'Haras had a valuable piece of property in Ireland that they rented out. Liam was trying to convince Connor to let him build a cottage on the property and live there."

"Resentment over such a discrepancy when it came to inheritance could have turned deadly," Jessica suggested, her eyebrows pinched with concentration. "I want to hear Liam's side of it, though."

"Me, too," Peter agreed.

Jessica straightened. "And I think I know where to track him down."

Pine Grove Animal Shelter was off the beaten path. It was larger than most shelters in a small town, having had many acres donated by an animal-loving resident years ago. They did the best they could with the land, allowing their rescues to have more space to roam than a lot of shelters were afforded.

Liam O'Hara volunteered at the shelter as part of his community service hours. Peter and Jessica found him with Pogo and another dog, a big St. Bernard. Pogo was nervous, but the St. Bernard lounged about nearby ignoring him. As Jessica approached, Pogo growled at her. She knew it was her and not the both of them because Pogo's big brown eyes were locked on her alone.

"I'll hang back," Jessica suggested, stopping. Pogo wasn't muzzled today and she didn't want to risk a bite. Not just for herself, but for what it would mean for Pogo.

"Sorry about that," Liam said as he stood. He gripped Pogo's leash tightly in one hand. "Pogo was abused by his owner when he was a puppy. She was a woman and ever since then, he just doesn't like women. Except Maeve."

Jessica nodded her understanding. "And you're working with him to build his confidence around other dogs, right?" Seeing Peter's raised eyebrows, she explained. "The St. Bernard is named Missy, and she's the shelter's mascot, so to say. She's got a very calm demeanor and works to be a calming presence for other dogs. I've worked with her before, too, before I got Charlie."

"We have some questions about the conflict you had with your brother," Peter said.

Liam got to his feet. "Let me stop you right there. I loved my brother. We didn't always get along and he could be a real jerk, but I loved him. Our parents decided to disinherit me when we were teens after I got caught up in the wrong crowd. My dad always said he meant for Connor and me to share the property fifty-fifty once I got my act together. I've been clean ten years."

Jessica nodded toward the shelter. "You still have court-appointed community service."

"From parking tickets I couldn't pay," Liam answered. "Got laid off my job and I haven't been able to find anything else. Yet."

"Connor wouldn't give you a job?" Jessica asked, surprised.

Liam looked at the ground. "Nah, and I can't blame him. Working at a pub as a recovering alcoholic isn't the smartest idea."

"But now you get it all," Peter prompted.

"Wrong." Liam shook his head. "Connor had a will. Maeve gets the pub and everything that comes with it. Fiona gets control of the family property in Ireland. She grew up with us and was practically our sister. Connor made a trust for me in case I need to go back to rehab, but otherwise, I'm Pogo's guardian and I've got a monthly share of the profits from the pub to take care of him. If I'm ever found to be neglecting him, though, it goes away."

"Is it enough to get by on?" Jessica asked, her brow furrowed.

Liam sighed. "It's enough so I won't have to live in my car. I think it was his way of looking out for me without having to outright say he was looking out for me."

Jessica nodded her sympathy. Liam looked pained at his brother's loss; she couldn't believe that he was the killer.

"Did Connor ever talk to you about Fiona being connected with your father's disappearance?" Peter asked.

"No. I mean, she was supposed to be up at the lake getting the cabin ready for us all to arrive. But she went off with friends instead." Liam shook his head. "I was always glad she didn't go up. Otherwise, she might have disappeared, too."

CHAPTER
FOUR

IT WAS GETTING LATE by the time they were finished interviewing Liam, so Peter and Jessica picked up Charlie and headed out to Peter's place. Sam was happy to see them return, and even happier that they brought Charlie with them. The two dogs dashed around the yard as Peter and Jessica sat on the front porch, going over the case.

"Connor has a journal entry here that just says 'She lied about the clover' and nothing else," Peter said, flipping through the book. It was a chilly evening and his breath puffed white into the air.

"Who lied?" Jessica asked.

"It doesn't say." Peter tucked the journal away. "I think there's something that Connor must have found that made him doubt Fiona's story about what happened the day his father disappeared. Tomorrow we should look through his ledgers. I bet we'll find something that Donnelly overlooked."

Jessica nodded as she pulled her coat tighter around herself. "I wonder if Liam will be open to introducing Pogo to Charlie. I feel so bad for him. But those bruises still make me so angry. I just wish I knew who caused them."

"Do you think it's connected with the murder?" Peter asked, his forehead furrowing.

"No," Jessica admitted. "But I can't see Connor kicking his dog, not after knowing the situation he rescued Pogo from. It couldn't be Liam or Maeve. Oh…" Her eyes widened as Sam grabbed a branch from the ground and nearly hit Charlie with it. "Oh, maybe I'm wrong! Maybe it wasn't from a kick at all."

"What do you mean?"

Jessica turned to him. "What if Connor took Pogo up to their cabin on the lake? If Pogo was running around, he might have jumped over a log and hit it or something."

Peter rubbed his chin. "If that's what happened, Connor must be investigating the cabin. But what happened after ten years to make him think he had a new lead in his father's disappearance?"

THE NEXT DAY, Peter arrived at the pub early. Jessica had to work at the vet clinic that day, but she promised to try to get Liam to bring Pogo in so she could better tell what caused his bruises. Maeve happily handed over the ledgers and books to Peter.

"Whatever will help you find the person responsible," she said, sniffing.

Peter nodded his thanks. Even though Maeve was a suspect—and on paper a good one—he didn't believe she would have hurt Connor. Her feelings for him were far too clear. Even if she had the means and motive because she inherited the pub, his gut said she wasn't the killer.

"Thank you, Maeve," he said. "Before you go, how long have you known the O'Haras?"

Maeve smiled. "I grew up in the apartment building just behind the pub. I got my first job here. I've known them for more decades than it's polite to ask a lady."

Peter smiled warmly at her. "So, you know that Fiona was raised with Connor and Liam?"

"Oh, yes. They were thick as thieves, the three of them. Right up until Liam started to make new friends with the wrong people if you know what I mean." Maeve shook her head, her expression growing cloudy. "I always thought it was Fiona who introduced him to that crowd. But she had the good sense to get herself away."

"What sort of crowd was it?" Peter asked curiously.

Maeve waved a hand. "Oh, you know. Drinking, drugs. They weren't anyone from Pine Grove. Now, if you'll excuse me. I have to start opening."

"Of course. Thank you, Maeve," Peter said.

As he started to go through the ledgers, he noticed one of the binders filled with papers looked off. One of the covers was slightly thicker than the other. Upon further inspection, he found a thin slit on the inside, near the spine. Several papers had been slid into the cover on the inside of the binder. The first one was a typed note telling Peter 'Nothing good will come of digging into the past.' The notes grew more and more threatening until the final one, which read, 'You'll regret not listening to me.'

A faint watermark lay in the corner of this final page; it was the image of a Celtic harp, the same image on the sign outside the pub.

Quickly, Peter checked other papers on the desk. A server's notepad caught his eye. It was the same paper and had the same watermark as the threatening notes. So, it had to be someone who worked at the pub who had typed up the notes. Connor must have known who it was.

Although, they were printed off. Someone had taken one of these notepads, separated the papers, and then printed them. Almost as if they were hiding their handwriting. So maybe Connor didn't know who it was exactly.

Peter skimmed through the journal, looking for any mention of the threatening notes. There was nothing about that, but one passage caught his eye.

Liam stopped by the pub today. Said he had a lawyer and threatened to dig into the will. Seems to think that I changed it after Da's death. Idiot boy. I don't believe him but I'm going to take a look myself. Maybe there's something in his old will I overlooked. Maybe someone had a motive to kill him. Maybe Liam did.

Peter pushed back from the desk and headed to where Maeve worked. "Maeve, who all has access to these notepads?"

Maeve glanced over. "Oh, everyone! We had a bunch of them printed and gave them away as novelties during the New Year."

"Liam has one?" Peter asked.

"Yeah. I gave him a job handing them out at the booth," Maeve said.

Peter arched one eyebrow. "Doesn't seem like Connor would have been happy about that."

"He wasn't. He was furious with me. But I figured it would give Liam enough money to get out of the cold and it wasn't near the booze." Maeve shook her head. "I just wish I knew what happened. It seemed like those two were finally mending patches, then all of a sudden Connor refused to see his brother again."

"Was that around the time he started to act paranoid?" Peter asked.

Maeve hesitated. "Yeah. It was."

Peter nodded grimly. So, Liam threatened to start looking into the will and Connor decided to do it himself. Then he started to receive threatening notes about not looking into the past. This was all connected to their father's disappearance, Peter just knew it. The question was, how?

CHAPTER
FIVE

JESSICA KNOCKED on Liam's door. When she contacted him, he suggested that she come to his place rather than him bringing Pogo to the clinic. It surprised her that he had a house at all. From the way he'd been talking, she expected to find him living out of his car. She supposed that it was just because he was strapped for cash. It was possible that he couldn't pay his parking tickets because all his money went to pay for his rent.

Liam answered, smiling. "Thank you so much for doing this, Dr. Stern. I'm concerned about Pogo's bruises, but I don't have the cash to take him back to his vet."

"Did Connor tell you what happened?" Jessica asked as she stepped in.

"He went up to the family cabin to make sure it was cleaned up or something. Pogo was playing in the snow drifts I guess and slipped or something," Liam answered.

Jessica nodded. Once she took a closer look, she would be able to confirm if Pogo's injuries were consistent with an accident or someone abusing him. She desperately hoped that it was an accident.

"He's in his kennel," Liam said, leading her into the living room. "I did what you suggested and gave him some sedatives on a treat just before you arrived."

Pogo lay in his cage, relaxed. He had a muzzle on again. He lifted his head and gave a half-hearted growl at the sight of her, but when Jessica turned her back, he relaxed again.

"I'll draw up some stronger stuff to give him a stick-poke with," Jessica said as she opened her medical bag. "So, this is your place? That your share of profits will pay for?" she prompted.

Liam leaned against a nearby chair. "Yeah. For now, at least. Fiona contacted a lawyer and asked for my trust to be released for me. She thinks we can work it out so that Maeve doesn't have to give me anything. I'll be able to use my funds to build that little cottage in Ireland and live there. A new start would be good for me."

Jessica filled a syringe. "I remember someone saying something about that. Why was Connor against that plan?"

"He... was worried that the stress of building a new life would make me fall into old habits," Liam admitted. "And I can't say I blame him, really. I've screwed up plenty."

Jessica hesitated a moment. She was here to focus on Pogo and determine if his injuries had anything to do with the case. On the other hand, Connor being out at the cabin did seem like it was relevant.

"Peter has found some evidence that Connor was looking into your father's disappearance again," she said, making sure her equipment was prepped. "Can you think of any reason why he would start into that again after ten years?"

Liam sighed. "Connor always believed something had happened. He used to say that he knew he could figure it out if he could find out what happened to this old brooch, I think it was. Honestly, the years after Da died were my worst. I don't recall much in that time. And Connor and I, we didn't talk about that anymore. It only ended in more fights. Does Mr. Myer think Da's disappearance has something to do with Connor's death?"

Jessica carefully used the stick prod to reach into the kennel and inject the sedation into Pogo's hindquarters. He yelped and snarled at her.

"I'm sorry, boy," she said in a soft, apologetic tone. "Can we go to a different room? He'll fight the sedative as long as I'm here."

Liam nodded. He led her to the kitchen and softly closed the door.

"Well? Does Myer think Connor's death is connected with Da's disappearance?"

"We don't know yet. It seems like he was looking into it, though," Jessica answered.

Before she could say more, a flurry of snarls and barks came from the living room. Both Liam and Jessica jumped in surprise. Then a woman's voice rang through the air.

"Shut up you mangy mutt!"

Liam groaned. "Fiona!" He yanked open the door. "Get in here. How many times do I have to tell you, you can't just stop in?"

"This is my house, you're just renting it," Fiona said as she stormed into the kitchen. She slammed the door and glared at Liam. "That dog is a menace! I told Connor years ago it needs to be put down. I will not allow it in this house, do you understand me?"

"Fio, I've been working with him for months," Liam said, lifting his hands. "He's made such good progress."

Fiona squinted at Jessica. "You. You're a vet. Can you put that animal to sleep?"

"I'm only here to take a look at his bruising," Jessica answered quietly.

Fiona rounded on Liam. "Really? You're wasting money on the dog? I'm out here trying to get your money to you and you're spending money like it grows on trees?"

Liam tensed. "You're only working so hard to get me that money because you know if I can build that cottage, your property values in Ireland will go up."

"Oh, and I suppose you having your own place where you don't have to pay rent is nothing, huh?" Fiona shook her head. "The more I listen to you, the more I think Connor was right. But here's the thing, Liam. Right now, I'm charging you below market value for this place. I told you no pets when you moved in and I mean no pets now. Get rid of the dog or find a new place to live."

"Fio—" Liam cut off. He ran a hand through his hair. "Fine. Fine, I'll be out by the end of the week. Connor left me the cabin on the lake. At least there Pogo won't have anyone trying to kill him!"

Fiona stared at him, her eyes widening. "The cabin? But... Liam,

I'm sorry. You won't have any heating or food or anything out there. No, I'll think about the dog. I only came to drop by this." She handed him a stack of papers. "For the lawyer."

She turned on her heel and marched out, her back straight. Jessica watched her go, the wheels turning in her mind. That had been... interesting. Was Pogo's aggression toward Fiona more than just his normal aggression? Or did he pick up on her hatred of him and respond in the same way?

CHAPTER
SIX

AT THE POLICE STATION, Peter watched in surprise as Donnelly fixed a cup of coffee. The police captain handed it to Jessica, then turned and made a second cup for Peter. After handing it over, Donnelly sat at his desk and slid an evidence bag toward Peter. He kept his hand over it, staring hard at Peter.

"You said you wanted a coffee, didn't you, Myer?" Donnelly demanded.

Peter sipped his coffee. The bold flavor was rich and deep. For the second time since coming to the station, he was surprised. He sniffed the coffee for any sort of trace of almond or odd scents. Why was Donnelly being so nice to him? It was quite the change from usual. The coffee smelled like coffee.

A pleased kind of smile passed briefly over Donnelly's face. He released the bag and Peter picked it up. A gold, clover-shaped brooch was in it.

"This was found in Connor's pocket," Donnelly said. "When Jessica called and asked me about a brooch, it jogged some memories. Connor was obsessed with finding a family heirloom. He kept saying that it should be with his father's things, but it was never found. He figured his father had had it when he disappeared, and was convinced if we could find it, it'd tell us what happened."

Peter studied the brooch. Though it was lovely, he couldn't see anything particularly special about it. "We don't know where Connor found it, do we?"

"Not a clue," Donnelly said with a nod.

Jessica sipped her coffee with a puzzled look on her face. "So, it's an old family heirloom that's been lost for ten years, and now we find it on Connor's body after he was murdered. What's the connection?"

"He said in his journal that 'she' lied about the clover. It could be this," Peter mused. He set the brooch down and drank a bit deeper into his coffee. "Whoever she was and what she lied about it. Fiona, Liam, and Connor were supposed to be up at the lake that day, yeah?"

"Just Fiona," Donnelly corrected. "Liam and Conner were going to come later. But Fiona went on a trip with her friends instead. I had several people come forward and confirm her story. They went on a trip out to the coast for a few days."

Peter hummed in thought. "Were these the same friends that Liam ended up getting mixed up with?"

Donnelly lifted one eyebrow. "Why?"

"Maeve said they were bad news. Maybe that alibi isn't as airtight as you thought."

"You think they were lying?" Jessica asked.

Peter shook his head. "I don't know. It'd be good to reach out to them again, though. Captain—"

"I can handle that." Donnelly nodded at the brooch. "You go ahead and take that. Show it to Fiona, Maeve, and Liam. Maybe seeing it will jog something for them."

Peter nodded. "I'll get right on that. Thanks, Captain."

Donnelly wrinkled his nose. "I'm only doing this because you'd get all involved in my case anyway. So don't fall all over yourself."

"Of course," Peter agreed. "Wouldn't think of it."

"MAYBE HE'S SICK," Jessica suggested after they left the station. "Could be a brain-eating parasite or something."

Peter laughed as he slid his hand into hers. "Let's hope not. The last thing we need is a zombie Captain Donnelly running around."

Jessica shivered. "Oh, that would be bad."

Peter leaned over to give her a peck on the cheek. They were back at the pub and went in together, hands still linked. It was one thing he adored about being with Jessica. Some people were uncomfortable with any sign of public affection, but Jessica was always relaxed when it came to walking and holding hands.

"Mr. Myer, Dr. Stern." Fiona greeted warily as they approached the bar. "What can I get for you? Or are you here on official business?"

"Official business," Peter said as he leaned against the bar. "We want to know what you know about this."

He pulled the brooch from his pocket and put it on the bar. He watched Fiona's face as her eyes widened. She leaned forward and touched it through the evidence baggie.

"Where did you get this?" she breathed.

"It was found on Connor's body."

Fiona picked it up and held it in the palm of her hand, her shoulders sagging. "This is a family heirloom. Every generation, one of the kids was picked as being the unluckiest and so the brooch was given to them. It's said to bring good luck. So, it was meant to dispel the bad fortune that clung to that child, you see. Once they were grown, it was meant to be given back to the O'Hara patriarch so he could give it to the next one."

"It was given to you as a child, wasn't it?" Jessica asked.

Fiona winced. "Yeah. After my parents died. Guess they thought there was nothing more unlucky than that. When I turned fifteen, I gave it back to Connor's dad. That was the weekend…"

"Connor seemed to be obsessed with finding it."

"Oh, he was. From what I understand, he took it from his dad's safe and gave it to Maeve to wear for some sort of pageant? Anyway, she said she lost it." Fiona shrugged as she put the brooch down on the bar. "I guess she must have lied. Just like she lied to Connor about…"

Peter leaned forward. "Lied to Connor about what?"

Fiona hesitated a moment before she brushed her hair over her shoulder and shook her head. "It's really none of my business. But you might want to ask her about all of the money that's been disappearing from the tills."

"Are you saying Maeve was stealing from Peter?" Jessica asked.

"I'm saying there was some funny business with the finances," Fiona said.

Peter nodded his thanks and tucked the brooch into his pocket again. If Maeve was stealing from the pub, then it gave her an even stronger motive. Enough to kill Connor, though? Perhaps... it might just be that his gut was wrong this entire time.

"THE BRUISES on Pogo's belly are consistent with getting hurt in the woods," Jessica said. "I contacted his vet, and there were abrasions on his belly that had bits of bark in them. I've never been more happy to be wrong." She took a bite of her burrito and shook her head. "Well, there's been a few times when I was afraid a client had cancer and I was wrong. But this is certainly a relief."

They were at the police station again. Sam and Charlie were quietly wandering around, sniffing things. Donnelly watched the two dogs with a distinctive unpleasantness. It was plain to see that he didn't like dogs, but when Jessica finished her piece, he shrugged.

"I could have told you that. Fiona O'Hara called me on Connor's dog a few times and it was plain as plain can be that Connor had an unhealthy attachment to the mutt." Donnelly leaned back and put his feet up on the desk. "That said, he was a better owner than a lot of people. Kept his dog under control and took precautions to make sure it'd never hurt anyone."

Peter sipped his coffee. How did the police captain make it so good? Did he get the expensive stuff that he hand-ground or something? "And that tells you that a person didn't abuse Pogo?"

"Sure does. If anyone had hit his dog, he'd have them brought up charges," Donnelly said firmly. "He's a sweet dog, too. Don't know what his problem with Fiona is."

"He was abused by a woman before he came to Connor," Jessica explained. "And Fiona was always aggressive toward him, so the dislike just grew from there."

Donnelly grunted. "So, we know that the dog didn't have anything to do with the murder. What did you learn about the brooch, Myer?"

"Fiona claims that Connor let Maeve borrow it and she lost it. Maeve claims that she never had it. I suspect that either Fiona never returned it to the O'Hara father or Maeve gave it back to him before he went up to the lake. Did you track down Fiona's old friends?" Peter asked.

Donnelly's frown deepened. "And that brings us to a rather sticky point. Four people said Fiona was with them that weekend. Turns out, the year after the disappearance, they were all in a car accident. Two of them died on the scene, the other ended up with extensive head trauma that left them unable to communicate, and the fourth... the fourth died three years after that from a drug overdose."

"So, we can't get any follow-up." Jessica wiped her fingers off on a napkin. "There's something else that we haven't talked about."

Both men turned to her expectantly.

"Maeve was the only one in the pub at the time of Connor's murder," she said. "She told us nobody came in or out during that time. So, who could have killed him but her?"

Donnelly smiled. "I wondered when you'd bring that up. A lock on the window was broken and we found scuff marks on the other side. Further, I talked with Maeve about the day and she admitted that she let Liam in earlier in the day and hid him in the basement, so Connor wouldn't see him."

Peter leaned his elbows onto the desk. "So, Liam was in the basement. And with Connor gone, he inherited the cabin, which he could sell if he wanted quick cash. Connor was blocking him from accessing the trust their father set up."

"And Fiona inherited the property in Ireland, where Liam wants to build and move to," Jessica added.

This certainly seemed like a solid case being built against Liam.

There were still missing pieces, though. How did any of it connect with the brooch? The threatening notes? And what about Fiona's suggestions that Maeve was stealing from the pub?

As he was lost in his thoughts, trying to puzzle it out, his eyes met Jessica's. Her eyebrows were drawn together, a serious expression on her face. Her eyes were sharp and clear and her mouth looked so kissable, Peter was distracted. Jessica was always beautiful, but he thought there was no time she was more beautiful than when she was thinking hard.

His heart skipped a beat. She was kind, gracious, elegant, and had a good heart. She loved to join him in figuring out cases. Her cleverness always impressed him. It had been a bumpy road for them to both admit that they had feelings for each other; and that was something he was determined not to repeat again.

"I don't know for certain, but I still think that Connor's death had something to do with that brooch," Jessica said. "Liam might have had motive but Maeve said he and Connor were starting to reconcile. He seems to be determined to turn his life around."

"Evidence doesn't lie, people do," Donnelly said.

Jessica nodded. "I understand that, Captain, but I have a theory. If you'll let me, I think I know how to find out who the real killer is once and for all."

CHAPTER
EIGHT

THAT NIGHT, Peter and Jessica had gathered the three suspects at the pub. Jessica had arranged for them to meet together to plan a town memorial to honor Connor's memory. Captain Donnelly joined them, looking dour as usual. Maeve poured everyone a round of sparkling, non-alcoholic cider. She seemed puzzled by Donnelly's inclusion. Liam and Fiona both seemed nervous.

"Thank you for coming together," Jessica said, smiling. Her stomach was a little woozy from the attention on her, but she fought not to show it. She just hoped she was right about this whole thing! "Now, I know Maeve was already planning a wake, but I thought since the O'Hara Pub is such a central gathering place, you might like help to arrange something larger for the town."

"That would be nice," Fiona said slowly, giving Donnelly a puzzled look.

Donnelly shrugged and looped his thumbs into his belt. "I liked Connor. Dr. Stern asked for me to help with the permits and whatnot, so I figured I'd best be here to hear whatever plans you think up."

He glared at Fiona as though daring her to contradict him. Well, it was a good thing to know that Peter wasn't the only person to be on the receiving end of that look. Jessica cleared her throat to draw everyone's attention back to her. This had to be done carefully, and being oddly combative wasn't going to help.

"Before we begin that, there's just one question we need to ask," Jessica said. "Maeve, when we were looking through Connor's financial records, we found some strange discrepancies. Some withdrawals were labeled as donations, but we can't find any record of where these donations went to. Can you explain it?"

Fiona looked a little relieved, Jessica noted.

Maeve sighed as she put her hands on her hips. "Connor had me make donations to the animal shelter. You see, it's the only place Liam has seemed to thrive, but Connor was too proud to say anything himself. With the town cuts, he was afraid the shelter would close and Liam wouldn't find a place as fulfilling to finish out his sentence... or potentially find a new career."

"He did that?" Liam's eyes were wide. "For me?"

Maeve nodded. She wrapped a sisterly arm around Liam's shoulders. "He loved you, Liam. Even when he was riding you about being a screw-up. He just wanted what was best for you."

"The donation returns aren't noted in your files," Peter said.

"That's because you didn't take the tax files. That's where we keep our receipts. You just have the ledgers showing the flow of money," Maeve answered.

Jessica nodded, brushing her hair behind her ear. "Right. So then there hasn't been any money that mysteriously goes missing from the tills?"

Maeve's forehead creased. "No. Why would there be?"

At this, Fiona snorted. "I know you've been palming tips, Maeve. You're supposed to share them with the whole staff, but you've been keeping them for yourself."

"Fio, the bartender keeps their tips. You know that," Maeve said, looking even more perplexed.

"You won't find any of that in the books or the manual," Fiona insisted. "I heard them arguing. She and Connor. Connor was telling her she couldn't keep the tips, she had to put them in the pool. But Maeve told him she wouldn't do it. In fact, the day before his death he told me that he was thinking of changing his will and leaving the pub to Liam instead!"

Gotcha, Jessica thought. She kept her expression bland as she asked, "Why would he give the pub to a recovering alcoholic? He wouldn't even give Liam a job there, in case the temptation grew to be too much."

Fiona shrugged. "Guess he would have changed it to come to me."

"No, he wouldn't," Liam argued. "He was in love with Maeve. The last time he and I got together he said he was planning on marrying her. Joked it was the best way to keep the O'Hara in the pub."

Fiona clenched her fists. "I'm an O'Hara. And I bet it was you who smashed him over the head with that whiskey bottle! I saw you sneaking out the basement window. You're the one who killed him, then staged it to look like an accident!"

"And how do you know that he was struck over the head?" Peter asked, his voice low.

Jessica sagged in relief. She'd done her part. Now it was time to leave it to Peter and Donnelly. She moved to Maeve and put an arm around her as she stared at Fiona, her eyes filled with betrayed tears.

PETER STEPPED CLOSER to Fiona as she stuttered over her words. Her face had gone pale. She knew she'd messed up, even if she didn't want to admit it. "You saw Liam come out through the window. You saw Connor down there and decided you'd go through the window, too. Maybe you weren't planning on killing him, but you didn't want Maeve to know you were there."

Fiona shook her head.

Donnelly cleared his throat. "We have video footage of you, Fiona. The store next door recently put a camera in the back alley. So why don't you tell us what happened?"

"I... I don't know what happened," she burst out. "I was going to tell him that Liam left through the window. I went in to prove that the lock was busted. I hoped to convince him to change the will... to cut

Liam out and leave me the cabin. But he had that blasted clover brooch. He kept demanding I tell him what really happened.

"I was so scared. So angry. I picked up the bottle and swung. I expected it to break over his head, like they do in the movies. But... but he fell. He wasn't breathing and I realized what I had done." Fiona covered her face with her hands. "If he didn't keep pushing..."

"Pushing about his father's death," Peter said softly.

Fiona nodded.

"You didn't give the brooch back to Connor's father, did you? You went up to the lake like you were supposed to. Those friends of yours were there, too." Peter filled in the blanks. "Connor figured out enough to leave clues in his journal. Connor's father found you there, didn't he? With your friends? You were drinking, that's clear. What else was going on? Drugs?"

"I suppose there's no point in hiding it anymore." Fiona sank into a chair. "One of my... my friends," she spat out the word, "had gotten his hands on some pretty hard stuff. And we stupidly decided to go out on the lake in a canoe."

Maeve covered her mouth, her eyes shining with tears. Beside her, Liam looked stricken.

"You killed my father?" he breathed.

Fiona lifted her head. "No. No, I didn't. The canoe capsized just as he arrived. He swam out to save us. But as he was getting us in, he got snagged on the canoe. It pulled him under. I was so high I didn't even know what was happening until I woke up the next morning. We... we hid his body. I left the brooch with him, I was so ashamed. Connor must have found..."

Peter nodded at Donnelly, whose face was more grim than normal. He pulled the handcuffs from his belt and approached Fiona. As he arrested her, Maeve and Liam hugged each other, starting to cry.

It was a terrible set of circumstances. Peter and Jessica shared sad looks. It was a heavy price to pay to know the truth. Hopefully, Liam and Maeve would find some peace in knowing that Connor loved them.

Sometimes, it was all that a person could leave behind... love.

EPILOGUE

MAEVE WIPED her hands on her slacks as she surveyed the crowd of happy, satisfied customers. The O'Hara Pub—her pub now—was still alive. If she was honest, she didn't think she would make it, being the owner and manager. The memories of all she shared here with Connor was so strong. She thought that the pain of losing him might make her lose any love she had for the pub.

Now, as she felt the warmth of Pine Grove's people around her, she was glad it hadn't turned out that way. Moving into the apartment above the pub was just one more thing she'd done to feel closer to the man she'd loved.

Peter Myer smiled at her as he took a seat at the bar. No doubt Jessica would be joining him. Those two were always together these days. And they made such a lovely couple, Maeve couldn't blame them.

"I'm glad to see you're back up and running," Peter said. "How are you doing?"

Maeve fluffed her wig. She'd gone with a green one tonight, in memory of the St. Patrick's day she never fully got to celebrate. "Oh, it's been a journey. I've been running around all evening. Checking the kitchen, pouring pints and the like. It's quite something to own O'Haras without having the name of it myself."

She smiled, but a small pang of sadness hit her stomach. She'd loved that family like her own and now things were never going to be the same. Liam stuck around—he'd put off his plans of moving to Ireland for now, though with Fiona on trial for murder, that land might go to him. Liam wanted nothing to do with the pub, and she understood why. On the bright side, he was making leaps and bounds with Pogo, and was even talking about getting a certificate to be a dog trainer.

"Speaking of," she said, then paused. "Or rather, while I'm thinking of it, remind me to thank Jessica for that fundraiser. Connor would have been touched that she did it in memorial for him."

Jessica had done a fundraiser for the local animal shelter. She'd called it 'A Penny for Pogo.' Connor loved that dog, and Maeve was happy that Jessica had gotten enough funds to keep the shelter open for other animals.

"She's meeting me here tonight, so you can tell her yourself," Peter said.

Maeve smiled to herself. Bingo! She'd been right on the money.

"Well, then, I'll just have to do that," Maeve agreed.

The pub buzzed with laughter and music. She made her round with familiar faces, thanking them for coming and accepting their heartfelt condolences. As she did so, she thought about Connor's wish to find out what happened to his father. They'd gone up to the cabin again, and found a map Connor had left leading to the body. Now father and son were lovingly interred in the family plot.

As Maeve saw Jessica enter the pub and make her way to Peter, she felt something beating in her chest that she hadn't felt for some time... hope. The pub was a symbol of so much. Once, it'd been her dreams of growing old with the man she loved. Now it was a new symbol, the sign that even when you felt like you couldn't keep going, you could find something worth holding onto.

This place is home, she thought, and she felt as though she could feel Connor standing next to her, smiling proudly at everything she'd accomplished.

She made her way back over to Jessica, who jumped to her feet to hug her.

"It was a roaring success. Thank you so much for helping," Jessica said before Maeve could thank her first.

Tears glinted in Maeve's eyes. "Thank you."

Jessica hugged her back tightly.

Maeve stepped back and wiped her eyes. As she did so, she spied Captain Donnelly in a corner booth. He waved her over and she headed to him, smiling. His grim expression didn't change.

"What can I get you, Captain?" Maeve asked. She'd draw a smile out of him tonight if it was the last thing she did.

Donnelly slid a picture toward her. "I want you to keep an eye out for me. If you see this man in town—especially if he hangs out with Myer—let me know."

Maeve frowned as she picked up the picture. It was a man with a round belly and an impressive beard. "Alright."

"And Maeve? Don't tell anyone I've got you looking out for him, hey?"

Maeve nodded, her frown deepening. What was this about? "Who is he?"

Donnelly stood and brushed off his hat. "A dangerous man," he said, not looking at her. "Goes by the name Marconi. Just keep an eye out, 'kay?"

He left the pub and Maeve watched him go, holding the photo still. Marconi. Who was he and why did Donnelly seem so nervous about him? She tucked the photo into her pocket. *I suppose only time will tell.*

The End

PRETTY DEADLY BLOOMS

A COZY MYSTERY

PROLOGUE

THE PINE GROVE GARDEN CLUB was all prepped for its annual Summertime Celebrations. Frankie Isles, three-year champion, was in her greenhouse, making sure all her plants were just right for the judge's committee, which would be arriving the next day. The greenhouse was a tall building, one that Frankie had spent a lot of time and money designing and having built. It was her dream, her life. Rows of her most precious plants filled the greenhouse, vibrant with greens, reds, pinks, blues, and a myriad of other colors.

Nobody had a better greenhouse display of flowers than Frankie. Nobody.

Somewhere beyond the glass walls of her castle, she heard the voice of her neighbor. Verna Timms, the crazy cat lady, was loudly talking with someone or another. Probably that no-good nephew of hers, the one that had all the tattooed friends.

Frankie glared in the direction of the Timms residence. That woman had been a thorn in her side since the day she moved in. Frankie didn't care if she was a licensed 'cat sanctuary' or whatever she called herself. Verna had no business taking up so much land with her stupid cats. They were always out and about, lounging in that ridiculous jungle gym cage that Verna called a 'catio.'

More than once, Frankie wanted to sneak over there, open up the doors that kept the cats locked up, and let the coyotes get them.

There was nothing Frankie Isles hated more than cats... except losing.

And last year she had lost. Gotten second place in the Summertime Celebrations. Second most beautiful greenhouse in Pine Grove. Second! And she knew she lost out because of Verna Timms' cathouse. Frankie had picked this plot of land because it abutted the natural forest and was the prettiest location in Pine Grove.

How was she supposed to know that a bunch of cats lived next door when she moved in? Nobody had warned her!

And now that it had cost her first place? Well... She picked up a flowering hydrangea. People didn't know it, but hydrangeas were actually poisonous. She smiled. A beautiful little plant... and it was going to win her first prize.

CHAPTER
ONE

PETER MYER WAS no stranger to murders in Pine Grove. For a town this small, it seemed there was an impossible number of killings that happened. What was unusual was that Captain Richard Donnelly, the police captain, would call him up and invite him to come join an investigation. But then, Donnelly had been relaxing his view on Peter lately. Maybe, after his many years of helping the police with various murder investigations, Donnelly was ready to put the past behind them.

He sighed as he stepped from his car, distracted by thoughts of his labrador, Sam. Sam had been lethargic lately and Peter had found a large lump on his back hind leg. He was trying not to worry about cancer. Right now, Sam was at the veterinary clinic with Peter's girlfriend, Dr. Jessica Stern. She was the only vet in Pine Grove and was currently slammed with work. She promised to take a look at Sam as soon as she could.

Luckily, Sam enjoyed hanging out at the clinic with Jessica's beagle, Charlie. The two were fast friends and had such chill personalities that they made good clinic dogs. They often worked in tandem to help keep the patients calm in the unfamiliar environment.

"Morning, Captain," Peter said, nodding to Donnelly as he stepped through the door to Frankie Isles' greenhouse.

A blast of heat hit him. Though there were large fans in the ceiling and several open windows, it felt like the tropics in here. He sucked in a lungful of the hot, moist air. Sweat already started to bead his forehead. Donnelly, in his uniform, seemed unaffected.

"Frankie Isles was found dead this morning by her neighbor, Verna Timms," Donnelly said. "Initial investigation showed Frankie has a bluish tint to her nails and lips."

"Poison," Peter said.

Donnelly nodded. "You worked on that crazy cat case a few years back. Verna Timms might seem like she's a doddering old lady—"

"Hey, that's not okay language to use," Peter interjected, frowning.

"I'm saying that's not what she is," Donnelly said, rolling his eyes.

Peter shook his head. "It's still not okay."

Donnelly rolled his eyes again. "What I'm saying is that Verna is sharper than she appears. She puts on a pretty good front for people, but she's far more clever than she lets on. Neighbors say she and the victim have had several public arguments over the past few weeks. I want you to go talk with her. She won't say a word to me."

I wonder why, Peter thought dryly. Several years ago, one of Verna's neighbors had been sabotaging her sanctuary. They stole several of her cats to get her shut down. This was despite her taking better care of the cats than many people took care of their children. At the time, Donnelly had outright rejected anything that was happening other than Verna being old.

He considered asking if that was the only reason Donnelly had invited him to join the investigation, but decided against it. Peter gratefully escaped the humid heat of the greenhouse and went to Verna's house.

Verna invited Peter to take a seat on the porch. "The police were banging on the door this morning and it startled the cats," she explained to him. She brought one of them out on a leash and harness. It sniffed curiously at Peter's hand when he reached to pet it.

"I hear you had words with Mrs. Isles," Peter said as he settled in his seat.

Verna's lips thinned. "You could say that, yes. She decided to go on a crusade to get my sanctuary shut down. Tried all sorts of nasty methods. I've been under a great deal of stress because of her. She blames me and my cats for why she didn't win first prize in the garden club last year."

Peter's brows furrowed. "Huh. Why did she blame you?"

"Because she can't admit that she got complacent and expected first prize to be handed to her without effort," Verna said grumpily. "She thinks that somehow my property impacted the judge's views of hers, even though nothing has changed since the previous years when she won first prize."

An SUV with tinted windows pulled up to the driveway. The familiar sight of Marconi stepped from the SUV, narrowing his eyes at Peter. Peter tensed in response. Though he had no hard proof, Marconi was involved with the mob. More than that, he'd been chummy with Peter's father; while Peter had taken his law degree to the FBI, his father had worked with the mob as their lawyer. It ended up with a strange almost friendly relationship between Peter and Marconi, though neither of them trusted the other.

"Aunt Verna," Marconi called as he came up the drive. "Are you okay?"

Verna smiled widely at him. "Yes, yes. There's just been some unfortunate business with Frankie."

Marconi stopped and gave Peter a baleful look. "Aunt Verna, I need to speak with you alone."

Peter got to his feet; it was clear he wasn't wanted anymore. "Thank you for talking with me, Verna. If you think of anything you might have heard or seen, please let me know."

"Of course," Verna agreed, patting his hand.

Making his way back to the Isles house, Peter felt the hairs on the back of his neck stand on end. He didn't need to look to see that Marconi was watching him. He imagined that Marconi would have that same distrustful, piercing look that Captain Donnelly did as he watched Peter return.

"Found this," Donnelly said. "What do you make of it?"

He held out a typed paper. Peter pulled on a pair of latex gloves before he took the paper. The words were bright and bold against the white background. *Drop out of the garden competition or you'll find something other than flowers in your greenhouse.*

It was unsigned.

Peter turned the paper over and frowned at it. "Someone didn't want to compete against her."

"Yeah," Donnelly said. "The question is, is it worth killing over?" He glared over Peter's shoulder toward the Timms house. "Or did Frankie Isles see something that she shouldn't have?"

CHAPTER TWO

"YOU THINK Marconi is involved in the murder?" Peter asked, surprised by this turn of events.

"Frankie Isles was having problems with Verna Timms. Now she just happens to have been murdered in her own greenhouse?" Donnelly shook his head. "We both know that Verna's 'nephew' there is involved in the mob. Don't deny it."

Peter gave Donnelly a critical look. "I wasn't going to deny it. He's been involved in plenty around here, but I've never had enough evidence for a conviction to stick."

Donnelly gave him a look that said, "Yeah, and your father working for his boss has nothing to do with it." Then he said it aloud. Peter tensed at the mention of his father. He hadn't known about his father's mob involvement until he moved back to Pine Grove. If there was one thing he wished he could ask his old man, it was that. How did he get involved?

Some things were just never going to be answered, though.

"Take this as your chance to prove once and for all that you're not dirty, Myer," Donnelly said. "If Marconi's involved, you'll be the one to bring him in."

Peter's brows furrowed but he only nodded.

"So, what do we know so far?" he asked, keeping his voice level.

"We know that Frankie Isles was growing many varieties of poisonous plants," Donnelly answered. "I ordered a tox screen to run so we can narrow it down and see if she was killed by her own plants. We'll have to find out how the poison was administered. She was too well-versed with her plants to chow down on hydrangea flowers."

"Hydrangeas are poisonous?"

Donnelly gave him an 'everyone knows that' look. "Yup. The symptoms don't line up with Frankie's death, though. I'm having the plants cataloged. In the meantime, I got something for you to look into."

Donnelly turned on his heel and led him into the house. Peter frowned at his back as they went to Frankie's study. There was clearly something more going on with Donnelly than he was saying, but what exactly was it? Did he think Peter was helping the mob?

In the office, Donnelly sat at the computer and pulled up Frankie's emails. "Frankie Isles was in a longstanding rivalry with another of the neighbors, Henry Clay. They've been fighting over the property lines between their places. Frankie claims she purchased the vacant lot between them while Henry claims it's part of his property."

"Is it enough to be a motive?" Peter asked, leaning over his shoulder.

"Probably not. On its own, that is." Donnelly pulled up a specific email. "But as you see here, Frankie was in the process of selling that lot, even though it was being disputed. Then add on the fact that Henry is also a member of the Garden Club. Every single year, he places just behind Frankie," he added as he leaned back in his chair. "Take a look at the name of the potential buyer."

Peter did so. His stomach sank. "Marconi."

Peter felt a chill run down his spine as he stared at the name. Marconi. The same Marconi whose involvement in the mob was an open secret in Pine Grove, the same Marconi who had an aunt just down the street. He wasn't stupid enough to think that this land buy was only for the sake of being closer to family.

"What would the mob want with that property, eh?" Donnelly demanded.

Peter turned to him. "One, I wouldn't have the first clue. Second, 'eh?' Are you Canadian?"

Donnelly scowled at him. "Don't change the subject. What do you think about this?"

"I think..." Peter leaned back on his heels. "That this is bigger than what small-town police can handle. And far bigger than a retired lawyer who does some sleuthing around town," he added, seeing Donnelly stiffen. "We're not equipped to handle the mob. And it certainly seems like Marconi could be involved here."

"He wasn't the only one interested in the property," Donnelly said, leaning back in his chair. "Seems to be that Frankie was trying to get a developer's bidding war going on. I want you to focus on Marconi, Myer. Get close to him and figure out what he wants with that property. If you get any indication he'd kill for it, then I'll get the feds involved. In the meantime, Henry Clay should have a few things to say about this potential sale."

Peter nodded, then hesitated. He met Donnelly's gaze, his brow furrowed. "Why are you involving me, Donnelly? You clearly don't trust me, and I can't say I blame you, not with my family history. But this seems..."

Donnelly glared at him before breaking eye contact. "Let's just say I have my reasons and keep it at that."

Was it a trap? Peter kept his expression blank as he nodded. Donnelly had seemed to soften over the years. This seemed like such a break in his character, though.

Regardless, Peter wasn't going to ruin the development by pushing too hard. Donnelly had given him enough of an answer for now. Peter had an 'in' with Marconi that Donnelly just didn't have. It hardly made Peter and Marconi friends, but Verna had a background in law enforcement. If Marconi was involved in something shady, her instincts should give him a heads-up.

That was if he could convince her to talk to him. It seemed this case had just gotten a lot more sticky.

CHAPTER
THREE

JESSICA SCRATCHED behind Sam's ears, grinning at his goofy face. He wagged his tail, leaning into her hands. The door to the office opened and Peter came in, looking worried. She'd already told him the good news over the phone, but she understood what it meant to have a pet that wasn't doing too well. All the symptoms Sam had were worrisome.

"The biopsy went great," she told Peter, straightening. "Sam handled it like a champ. All I saw was fatty tissue inside, but I'd like to take off the lump and send it for analysis just in case."

Peter patted Sam's head. "Would that explain why he's been lethargic lately?"

"No," Jessica said slowly. That was quite the mystery still. "I've run bloodwork and everything seems normal. Have you changed his food or treats at all?"

"No." Peter crouched next to Sam and scratched behind his ears. "He's just acting... I don't know, like he's depressed."

Jessica nodded slowly. "How about I come over tonight with Charlie and see how they interact? And we can take a look at his food, see if the company changed their formula."

Peter grinned up at her. "Any excuse to get me to cook supper, huh?"

"Of course!" Jessica laughed.

"Can he stay with you for a while longer?" Peter straightened. "Donnelly asked me to help with an investigation. I'm about to head over to the Pine Grove Garden Club Center, and I don't want to drag him all over the place while he's not feeling well."

Jessica glanced down at Sam. He was perfectly animated right now, wagging his tail and his eyes bright. She nodded. "Sure thing. I'll put him with Charlie."

It was different having the two of them at the clinic than at home. They both seemed to know that the clinic meant 'work' and so tamped down on their natural enthusiasm. She really wanted to see the two of them in a relaxed setting. She had a suspicion as to what this might be. And after Peter kissed her and left, and Sam flopped to the ground whining, her suspicions grew stronger.

"It's okay, buddy," she said soothingly, petting his silky ears. "Let's go see Charlie."

HENRY CLAY WAS a middle-aged man with a heavy brow and brilliantly blue eyes that seemed too round and boyish for his face. He greeted Peter with a nervous smile which quickly disappeared as soon as Peter brought up Frankie Isles.

"She was a dirty snake in the grass," Henry declared, clenching his hands into fists. "She was all smiles and sweetness to your face, but if you turned your back on her, bam! She'd get you. She sabotaged my garden, did you know that? The year before last, I had the most beautiful hydrangeas. But she made a complaint to the city about them encroaching on her property and had them all cut down!"

"Is that where the dispute over your property line came from?" Peter asked evenly.

"It's the reason she started claiming that empty lot," Henry said, shaking his head in disgust.

Peter made a note in his booklet. Odd that she would cut down hydrangeas one year only to start growing some herself. He'd have to check the city logs to ensure that it was, in fact, Frankie who had caused them to be cut down.

"And you're aware that hydrangeas are poisonous?" he asked coolly.

Henry laughed. "Oh, of course! Anyone who knows plants knows that. I have stories from growing up about my mother putting hydrangeas on her wedding cake. Everyone got sick. People don't stop to think that not everything in nature is meant to be consumed."

"Did you know Frankie had put the lot between your properties up for sale?" Peter asked.

Henry's eyes widened. "She did? That... that.... Dishonest woman!" He exploded. "I saw it went up for sale and I was thinking of putting a bid on it to show her what's what. I bet she's put half of my property in that sale, too! Excuse me, I need to call my lawyer."

He stalked away as he whipped his cell phone from his pocket. Peter couldn't help but be glad he wasn't the lawyer that was about to receive an earful about Frankie's land-related schemes... if they were schemes at all. Peter made a note to stop in at the town hall. He needed to know for sure if there was an official dispute to the property lines or if it was just Henry.

As he did so, a young woman sidled up to him. She was the youngest person in the club that he'd seen. While most of the members were middle-aged or older, well-established in their lives, she couldn't have been more than twenty. He had assumed she was here with a parent or grandparent.

"I hope you don't mind, but I overheard your conversation with Henry," she said, blushing as she spoke. "My name is Kelly Bradford. You're investigating Mrs. Isles' death, yes?"

"I am. Did you want to tell me anything?" Peter asked, keeping his voice low and soothing. The young woman twitched and bounced on the spot, as though it was taking a lot of energy not to bolt. She wrung her hands as she nodded. Peter guided her a little way from the others at the club, to lower the risk of being overheard and interrupted. "What is it?"

Kelly bit her lip. "Mr. Clay isn't the only one Mrs. Isles had trouble with. The first year she won, she was originally going to take second, but the first-place winner suddenly withdrew from the competition. Everyone thought that Mrs. Isles must have been blackmailing her."

"Who was this person?" Peter asked.

"Well... I don't have any proof that it was blackmail," Kelly said quickly. "I don't want to get anyone in legal trouble."

Peter smiled at her. "That's quite alright. I'm just getting a sense of things right now. Who was it?"

"Verna Timms," Kelly said. "After she withdrew from the competition, she quit the Garden Club altogether."

CHAPTER
FOUR

AS PETER WAS HEADED BACK to Verna Timms' place, he got a call from Captain Donnelly, telling him to come to the station. Peter agreed. No small part of him was relieved to have the excuse to put off confronting Verna. She was a friend, and despite her ties to Marconi, he thought she was someone who would do the right thing.

He was starting to have doubts, though. Someone with her background was capable of committing a murder and getting away with it. Although, if she was the killer, he would have expected that she would have staged it to look like an accident. Regardless, he wasn't looking forward to the conversation he was going to have to have with her.

"Frankie was killed with a combination of ingested and aerosol poisons," Donnelly told him when he came in. "There are a few plants in her collection that give off a certain sort of spore that affects respiration. We found them in a separate, closed-off space of the greenhouse, but the spore count within their space was lower than it ought to have been, and the spore count in the main greenhouse was higher."

Peter grimaced. They'd been walking around the greenhouse without any protective gear.

Donnelly caught his look. "I've had my people who processed the scene checked out. None of them had any effects, so you're in the clear since you didn't spend as much time in the greenhouse."

"Thanks," Peter said with a nod. "I take it that this spore space in the greenhouse was closed when you found the body."

"It was, so we're dealing with someone who closed the doors after Frankie died. We checked for prints, but came up empty."

Peter crossed his legs. "You said it was a combination poisoning?"

"Right." Donnelly slid a file across the desk to Peter. "The spores on their own wouldn't have been enough to kill her. They would have caused some respiratory distress, but she was killed very quickly. She ingested a poison derived from other plants in her greenhouse. We found bits of the plant in her homemade tea mixes. When added together, she didn't stand a chance."

"So, someone had to have access to her greenhouse to pull this off."

Donnelly viewed him for a moment before he shook his head. "Opening up the spore storage, yeah. But the other plant? It's a common plant found through the Garden Club. Everyone's put it in their collections since the winner of the annual competition grew it in her garden four years ago."

This meant that the killer could have gotten that plant anywhere, and only had to break into Frankie's greenhouse once. As Peter mulled this over, he realized that it didn't even have to be someone in the Garden Club at all. All they had to know was how to hide the poison in Frankie's tea.

Which, in turn, indicated someone who could sneak into Frankie's house without her knowledge.

"I don't suppose there were any reports from Frankie about someone breaking into her house?" Peter asked, reluctant to find out where this was heading.

Donnelly shook his head, his expression grim. "Nothing recent. She called in about six months ago, saying someone was creeping around her yard, but we haven't heard anything since. Most of her calls were complaints against Verna Timms."

Peter frowned. "Could it have someone casing the place?"

"Possibly," Donnelly admitted. "But if they were, they were patient. Six months is a long time to go between casing out the place and stepping up to murder. But we both know my feelings on the matter. So have you heard about any problems Frankie might have had with Marconi directly?"

"No." Peter leaned back, his frown deepening. "Not directly. There's been plenty of other problems between Frankie and Verna, though."

He summed up what Kelly had told him about Verna taking first place in the Garden Club only to suddenly withdraw, leaving Frankie to claim first prize. Donnelly's usually grumpy face grew even grumpier as Peter finished up.

"I doubt even the likes of Marconi would resort to murder just because his aunt was offended," he said.

"Frankie was threatening her cat sanctuary," Peter pointed out. "And he has a great deal of loyalty toward his aunt. Verna loves those cats. She's getting older, though, and the stress of having the town called on her repeatedly by a neighbor who only had to make a call every once in a while could have worn thin."

"I see your point, but I still think a more likely motive has to do with that property," Donnelly said.

Peter scratched his chin, thinking. It was more logical, yes. But that was because Marconi was Donnelly's prime suspect. He didn't know about Verna's background or her capabilities. Did Peter bring it up? Verna had lived a quiet life since her retirement. It would be a shame to disrupt it all if it turned out that the murder had nothing to do with her.

On the other hand, it would be worse if she was the killer and got away because Peter didn't share all his information.

With a ragged sigh, he looked up at Donnelly again. "There's something you should know about Verna Timms. She worked for the FBI. She was known as Shadowcat, a highly skilled agent whose ability to solve crimes borders on the mythological. She's figured out cases tougher than this. I suspect she worked for the CIA as well."

Donnelly stared at him blankly. "Verna Timms?"

"Yes. We can't discount her as a suspect."

"Verna Timms… worked for the FBI?" Donnelly repeated.

Peter nodded.

Donnelly leaned back in his chair. "Huh."

"I'll call Tiff, an old colleague," Peter said. "Maybe there's something in her record that will help us build the case or clear her."

"And her secret name was Shadowcat?" Donnelly asked, seemingly not hearing a word Peter was saying.

Peter sighed and stood. "I'm going to go talk with her."

Donnelly waved a hand. "No wonder she has so many cats... she's one of them..."

Peter shook his head as he left the station. Hopefully, he hadn't just broken the police captain.

CHAPTER
FIVE

PETER PULLED up to the Timms residence, his stomach tightening at the sight of the cheerful little home with its closed-in patio. Several of the cats lounged in various spots within their safe space, watching him with sleepy eyes. He was glad to see that it was only Verna's car in the driveway. This was going to be a prickly enough situation without involving Marconi in it.

Taking a deep breath, Peter walked up to the door and knocked. After a few moments, it opened to show Verna. She smiled at him warmly as she invited him in. Peter nodded his thanks. Inside the house smelled clean and fresh. Verna took good care of her cats and home. Verna shut the door behind him and ushered him to the living room. A hairless cat watched him from within the warm embrace of a fluffy black and white cat.

"Can I get you anything to drink?" Verna asked Peter.

"No, thank you. Captain Donnelly asked me to stop by, to see if you had any new information or if you remembered seeing anyone near Frankie's place over the last few weeks."

Verna frowned at him. Nothing escaped her sharp gaze. "Are you saying I'm a suspect, Peter?"

There was no point in denying it. "Yes. You and your nephew both."

"I see." She folded her slender arms, her lips pressing together into a thin line. "Then how can you believe anything I tell you? I could be lying to throw you off the track."

"Or you could be innocent and provide valuable witness," Peter answered swiftly. "Either way…"

Verna hummed quietly to herself. "Either way, I really ought to have a lawyer. I know what these situations can turn into. Words can so easily be twisted around to suit a presupposed outcome."

Peter shook his head. "I'm not assuming anything, Verna. Though you are right. A lawyer will protect you either way."

She gave him a small smile. "I never cared much for lawyers. Except for you. There's not much I can tell you about Frankie Isles that you won't hear from anyone else. She's famous in the neighborhood for her screaming matches. She's been recently feuding with Henry Clay, but last week she nearly had herself banned from the grocery store by screaming at poor Leah Peabody."

"You and Frankie were rivals when it came to the Garden Club, too, weren't you?" Peter asked.

Verna's eyebrows stitched together. "Where did you hear that?"

"At the club. They said that you should have won several years ago but you suddenly withdrew, after you were chosen to be first place," Peter prompted.

"It was a long time ago. I realized that I was spending far too much time on that club and it was making me miserable. I didn't care about winning, and Frankie was so vengeful about it, I didn't want the headache." Verna sighed. "I only wish that had been the end of it. Instead, she's remained a headache all these years. But I did my best to avoid her," she added, a slight defensive note to her voice. "I wouldn't go so far as to kill her. My nephew has been looking to get me a new place, with more land so I can expand my sanctuary."

Peter frowned. "Expand?"'

Verna nodded. "Just ask Jessica. There's been a record number of abandoned animals in Pine Grove this year. It's awful." Her jaw clenched and tears came to her eyes. "Why would I be bothered about Frankie when I'm planning on moving anyway? I just had to wait her out."

"We have evidence Marconi was looking to buy the empty lot between Frankie and Henry's places," Peter said. "Was that where he was looking to help you move?"

"No."

Peter searched her, looking for any sign that she knew something that she wasn't saying. Verna's shoulders stiffened under his scrutiny. He leaned back against the sofa, frowning at her. "Why would he be interested in that property?"

"I don't think he is. I think…" Verna sighed. "I think he was stringing Frankie along. Making her hold out for the hope that he'd buy it at more than it was worth, make her dismiss other offers, then pull the rug out from under her and no longer be interested."

"Do you really believe that?" Peter asked quietly. There was something about the way she was holding herself and in her tone that made him think she was trying to convince herself.

Verna gave him a hard look, the agent she had once been shining though. "Sometimes you have to believe family, Peter. He's the only person I have left. What am I going to do, assume the worst and throw him out? Who am I going to have if I lose him?"

That certainly sounded as though it was on the brink of being a confession. Verna didn't believe what she was saying, but she wasn't going to admit it. Peter tapped his fingers on the arm of the sofa. If he asked outright, she wouldn't say if she believed Marconi had killed Frankie. So, what could he do from here?

"I will say, it seems as though Frankie was starting to catch on. To his scheme, I mean," Verna added. "She was acting rather erratically lately. She was always tightly wound but these last few weeks, she's been paranoid. Kept ranting about being sabotaged, how people were trying to steal her land."

"Could it be related to her troubles with Henry Clay?" Peter asked, interested. "That she thought he was trying to steal it from her?"

Verna shrugged. "I can't say. I hadn't exchanged more than a few words with Frankie these last few years. We didn't get along, you see."

She gave him an ironic smile at that. Peter laughed, though he was still ill at ease. Perhaps Frankie had found out Marconi was stringing her along... or maybe there was something even more insidious at work in Pine Grove.

CHAPTER
SIX

PETER SMILED AT JESSICA, happy that the long day was over. He didn't feel as though he was closer to figuring out who killed Frankie Isles, but he was looking forward to an evening with his girlfriend. He gave her a light kiss as he set down the potato casserole onto the table. The smell was divine and his stomach rumbled hungrily. Sam and Charlie lay sprawled out on the beds to the side of the room, exhausted after a very intense game of tag.

"Sam looks like he's perked up a lot," Peter observed.

"Oh, yes. He's been full of vinegar," Jessica agreed as she took her seat. "And I have a theory about that."

Peter started to dish up the food. Getting to the bottom of the mystery that was Sam would be very useful. "Does he need medication? Maybe I'm taking him on too long of walks..."

Jessica laughed, amused by his worries. She smiled gently at him. "Actually, I think that's the opposite of the problem."

"What do you mean?" Peter frowned at her. Sam had been so lethargic lately, he thought perhaps the dog was just too exhausted all the time.

"Over the winter you stopped taking him out as much because you were worried about the cold, right?" Jessica prompted.

Peter nodded. "And that's when he started to act like he was sick."

"So, you've been keeping him home, trying to help him recover," Jessica continued. "But look at the way he was bouncing all over the place with Charlie today. I don't think there's anything wrong with Sam, except that he's lonely. He's used to going everywhere with you, so when you stopped taking him out as much, he got lonely and bored."

Peter sat there, stunned at this revelation. It was true. Ever since he got Sam, they'd spend pretty much the entire day together. Even when working a case, Sam was never too far away. But lately he'd been leaving Sam at home more often, out of concern that there was just too much excitement and Sam wasn't feeling well.

"So, I'm actively making it worse," Peter said. An awful feeling of guilt swamped his stomach. "Oh, Sam, I'm so sorry,"

Sam lifted his head and wagged his tail once. "Woof."

Jessica reached across the table and took his hand in hers. "Don't feel bad, Peter. You've had a lot on your mind and you were just trying to help him out. Don't beat yourself up over something you didn't know. Sam is a happy, healthy dog and he loves you."

"I know he does," Peter said, smiling over at Sam. "He's been the best dog a man could ask for." That reminded him of the lump and he took a deep breath. "Did you get the results from the lab on that biopsy?"

"Not yet, but it should get here in a day or two. Do you want me to take it off in the meantime?" Jessica asked. "It's a pretty straightforward surgery, even if it's not strictly necessary."

Peter nodded firmly. He had the means to get the lump removed. Even if it wasn't cancer, he noticed sometimes the placement seemed to bother Sam. "Best to get it off and done with. Then I don't have to worry anymore."

"I'll find a place in my schedule to do it, then," Jessica assured him.

"And tomorrow, you're coming with me everywhere," Peter promised firmly.

"Woof," Sam said, giving him a doggy smile.

Both Jessica and Peter laughed. Jessica squeezed his hand as they started to eat. She spent some time telling him about her day. Peter listened intently, laughing along with her during the funny stories. He privately thought Jessica should start writing these things down. Her stories were just so entertaining.

They were almost ready for dessert when a fierce pounding came on the door. Peter frowned as he went to answer it.

"Myer, I need to talk with you," Marconi's voice came through the door. "Open up."

Peter gestured Jessica back as Sam and Charlie started to bark. He didn't believe that Marconi would announce himself like this if he was here to hurt anyone, but he couldn't be certain. He opened the door, keeping his body in the crack to keep Sam from poking his head through.

Marconi folded his thick arms and narrowed his eyes at Peter. "What's this nonsense about you thinking my aunt killed Frankie Isles?"

"Let's step out here to talk," Peter said, keeping his voice even.

"She didn't hurt anyone," Marconi insisted as he backed up, letting Peter through the doorway.

Peter shut the screen door behind him. Sam and Charlie, both standing in the doorway, whined. Marconi cast them a narrow-eyed look.

"I'm not going to hurt your dog or Dr. Stern," he grumbled. Then he grimaced, shifting on the spot. "Or you, Myer. I'm not here to do anything but talk. Okay? So you don't have to be so..." He waved his hand distractedly. "Aunt Verna wouldn't hurt a fly. So she had problems with Frankie Isles, that's why I was looking to get her moved."

"And why were you interested in buying another property in the area?" Peter asked quickly.

Marconi narrowed his eyes, though he didn't look surprised at the question. "I'm retiring from my current... business. I want to get into real estate. Gotta fund the retirement somehow and Pine Grove is an up-and-coming place with all the work done into promoting its natural beauty."

Peter studied him. There was something shifty about the way he was speaking that indicated it wasn't the entire truth. "Your aunt seemed to think you were just messing with Frankie."

"Might have been part of it," Marconi admitted.

"You'll understand why I ask this. Where you were the night she was killed?"

Marconi's lips quirked into something like a smile. "I was with some friends at a poker game. And no, none of them will provide an alibi. But I didn't kill Frankie Isles. I had no reason to. Maybe you should be looking at the Garden Club more closely. The first prize money can be quite… motivating."

CHAPTER
SEVEN

HENRY CLAY'S garden was magnificent. Unlike Frankie, who relied on her greenhouse to grow tropical, flowering plants, Henry had focused on native flora. The bushes and flowers might not be as dramatic as Frankie's, but they were still beautiful and the way Henry did his landscaping was very impressive. The only thing that marred the effect was the line of hewn-down hydrangeas bordering the property.

"I don't know what you want to talk to me about," Henry said as he used a pair of pruning sheers to shape a hedgerow along the back of his property. "I told Captain Donnelly everything. I didn't see anything. I was out of town when Frankie, bless her soul, was taken from us. There's nothing else I can tell you."

"Actually, I'm interested in the property disputes you and Frankie were having," Peter answered easily. "You see, I know of a party interested in the adjoining lot, and I have reason to believe that they may have had motive to see Frankie dead."

Henry's eyes widened. "Really?"

Peter nodded once. "You asked to have surveys done to establish the property line, yes?"

"Yes. Several times," Henry said, scowling. "But did it ever happen? No! It never happened. I think Frankie must have been bribing them. She won the first prize money three years in a row, you know," he added, "and I would have won if she hadn't cut down my prize hydrangeas."

"She didn't win last year," Peter said slowly.

Henry smirked. "Oh, no she didn't. And she blames Verna Timms, if you can believe it! Really, it's because she got lazy. I didn't participate last year. Otherwise, I would have won and then she couldn't blame the neighborhood. See this? This is going to get me first prize this year."

He crouched next to a flowering rosebush. As Peter approached, the sweet scent wafted toward him. He breathed it in, surprised. In his experience, roses either looked beautiful or smelled beautiful. It was rare to find a plant that did both.

"And it's right next to my house. Let's see Frankie wreck this and use the excuse of it encroaching on her territory!" Henry smirked in a self-satisfied way as he straightened.

"Winning the annual Garden Club prize is very important to you, isn't it?" Peter asked, his voice low.

Henry nodded. "I've been chasing first prize for over a decade. I always land second place. It wasn't so bad when Verna was the one beating me out. She did wonders with her garden! And she was always friendly about it, always willing to step in and help me out if I had to leave town for a few days. Frankie was a right pill about it all."

Peter took a moment to secure that to memory. "Is there a reason you didn't participate in the competition last year?"

"That." He pointed toward Frankie's house. "She was causing me so much stress, my hair started to fall out. I couldn't concentrate. And I was working hard to get my place back into shape after she destroyed my prize hydrangeas."

"I'd be mad if someone messed with my property, too," Peter said sympathetically.

Henry wiped his eyes. "You should have seen them. They were the most beautiful little shrubs you'd ever seen. Just breathtaking. And when I saw that Frankie was including hydrangeas into her gardens... it just about broke my heart."

"Did you see anyone unusual hanging around her place?" Peter asked.

Henry tapped his chin as he thought about it. "You know what? I think I did. A couple weeks ago, I saw a strange man leaving her greenhouse. He was about this tall and had a bit of a gut, if you know what I mean. It was dark but I thought it might be that nephew of Verna Timms."

"He was considering buying the empty lot." Peter nodded toward the vacant property.

For a moment it seemed that Henry floundered, but he quickly shrugged. "Oh. Well, that explains it, then. I thought they might be seeing each other."

"Seeing each other?" Peter repeated.

"Oh, yes. He often was in and out of her house when she wasn't home. I thought it was a bit strange, but I didn't know what their relationship was. I figured they were trying to keep it a secret from Verna," Henry said flippantly.

Peter jotted it down in his notebook. Marconi and Frankie, seeing each other? It seemed impossible. Nothing in Marconi's demeanor had suggested that they were a couple. Henry had clear motive with his hydrangeas. Peter had never known someone to hold such a grudge against another person over plants. This wasn't just about disputed property boundaries.

If it was Henry, though, how did he do it? Peter fought to keep his face clear of suspicion.

"Actually, there's a few strange things in Frankie's greenhouse that I could use your opinion on," he said casually. "Captain Donnelly dismissed it out of hand, but I think our killer might have been smarter than Donnelly gives him credit for."

Henry shrugged. "Sure thing, I can take a look. Right now, though, I'm due at a meeting at the Garden Club. We're discussing whether to hold this year's competition. Some members think we should put a pause on it, in honor of Frankie."

"Mind if I tag along?" Peter asked quickly. Marconi's advice to look into the Garden Club still rang in his ears. He'd been so focused on

Marconi and Verna that he'd forgotten there were others who might have reason to wish Frankie harm.

"It's really boring," Henry said doubtfully.

Peter grinned. "Don't worry. I'm a lawyer. I can handle boring."

CHAPTER
EIGHT

THE GARDEN CLUB, as it turned out, did very little to move the case forward. The vast majority of the meeting was dedicated to arguing over whether a 'rock garden' should count as a garden. The hot-button topic nearly brought people to blows. The most enlightening aspect was when the vote to halt this year's competition came up, and it was a resounding 'no.' Nobody suggested any other options to honor Frankie's place in the club, either. Clearly, she wasn't a well-liked member of the community.

By the time the meeting was over, Sam was ready to be picked up from his surgery—Jessica had had a cancellation and so was able to take off the lump.

Sam wagged his whole body when Peter came to the clinic. He leaned against Peter's legs and gave him an adoring look. Nearby, Charlie rolled onto his back and started snoring.

"Everything went fantastic," Jessica told Peter. "I took a closer look at the mass after I removed it. Fatty lipoma. Sam's going to be just fine."

Peter knelt beside his dog and pet him. The 'cone of shame' looked ridiculous on him, but he'd only need to wear it for a few days. Peter got the meds he'd need and listened carefully to the instructions for keeping the surgery site clean, and what warning signs to look out for.

"I think that's it," Jessica said, rubbing Sam's silky ears. "But if you need anything, don't hesitate to call."

"Thanks."

Jessica kissed his cheek. "I have to make some farm calls, but want to come over to my place tonight? You can update me on the case and maybe there's something I can do to help," she suggested.

Peter nodded. "Sounds great!"

Which was how he found himself later that night sitting in Jessica's living room, Sam nestled up against his side and Charlie's claws tippy-tapping as he wandered around the kitchen in search of a morsel Jessica might have dropped. Jessica sat on the floor with Peter as they went through Frankie's meticulous records of every dispute and perceived slight she'd received from the Garden Club.

"I can see why Donnelly gave you this," Jessica said as she sipped an herbal tea. "It's all so… boring."

Peter chuckled. He'd gone through his stack of journals noting down any time Verna or Henry was mentioned, but was keeping an eye out for any recurring problems. "She certainly thought everyone was out to get her, didn't she?"

Jessica nodded. "Some of these are surprisingly understandable, though. I mean, listen to this, 'Henry Clay tried to have me dismissed from the competition on the grounds that it's supposed to be a garden club and I have a greenhouse. I had to point out that he started his plants in a greenhouse nursery to get him to back down. He gave me a note after the meeting telling me to watch my back.' If we can find that note, it will certainly be incriminating."

"Does she say what the note said precisely?" Peter asked, leaving forward.

"Drop out of the garden competition or you'll find something other than flowers in your greenhouse," Jessica read.

"We found that note," Peter said excitedly. "Donnelly picked it up on the day of the murder. So now we have a threat linked to Henry Clay."

Jessica put aside the journal she was reading. "Do you really think that he is the killer?"

Peter thought over the question, a slight crease between his brows.

"If I'm honest, I'm not sure. I feel as though I've been going back and forth on this one. Maybe I'm putting too much pressure on myself. The fact is, when I look at it from a step back, Marconi had no real reason to kill Frankie. If she saw something related to the mob, he wouldn't have gone through the elaborate ploy to poison her. Certainly not setting it up six months in advance."

"Wait, six months? You think that whoever poisoned her set her up that early?" Jessica asked, her eyes widening.

That was right. He hadn't told her much about the case, since their times together had been dominated by worrying about Sam. Peter pulled out his notebook and checked his notes.

"Six months ago, Frankie called Donnelly about a supposed prowler," he said. "Donnelly asked the pathologist to do some tests on Frankie's systems and from the results, we can tell that she started to be poisoned around that time. Now, the oral poisons weren't enough to kill her, but they were enough to weaken her system. It wasn't until the cabinet in her greenhouse was left open for the spores to escape that it tipped her over."

Jessica rubbed her chin thoughtfully as she absorbed that. "I see. So, whoever set her up had to have a good knowledge of plants."

Peter nodded. "Not only did they have to know what plants to mix with her tea, but also how to do it in a way that wouldn't alter the taste of it."

"Let me check her journal from six months ago," Jessica said, reaching for it. She flipped through the pages and nodded when she arrived at the right spot. "Right here. Someone was creeping around the greenhouse. There were chips of paint taken off the door. I'm sure someone tried to break in but nobody believes me. I'm going to get a new lock put in. Henry Clay says I can take an old keypad of his. He told me that the surveys have come back and that I was right all along."

Peter lifted his head. "Wait, what? When I talked to him, Henry said that the surveys weren't coming in at all."

Jessica showed him the page. Peter flipped through the rest of it, his heart sinking. That was the last time Henry Clay was mentioned.

Instead, it suddenly turned to all sorts of problems Frankie was having with Verna.

"I found cat poop in my garden," he murmured, reading out loud. "This does it. Verna Timms keeps saying that she keeps her cats locked up, but clearly, she doesn't. If this doesn't stop, I'm going to open up that cage and let the coyotes get them."

Peter lifted his head and stared at Jessica, who stared wide-eyed back. That was it. He found the last piece of the puzzle.

CHAPTER
NINE

"HE PUT cat poop in her greenhouse gardens before he poisoned Frankie," Peter said. "There was no sign of forced entry, which means whoever got into the greenhouse knew the code on her lock. If we can prove that he knows the code, we can prove he was the one who opened that cabinet."

Captain Richard Donnelly squinted suspiciously at the papers Peter presented to him the next day. Sam sat happily at Peter's feet, his eyes bright. He didn't even seem to be bothered by the 'cone of shame' he wore. Donnelly sorted through the papers, then pushed them aside. He leaned back in his chair, lacing his fingers over his stomach as he turned that suspicious look on Peter.

"How do I know you're not setting Henry Clay up?" he asked, his voice flat.

Peter was expecting this. "Have you looked more into Marconi's actions here in town? About what properties he's interested in buying?"

Donnelly sucked on his teeth, then said, somewhat reluctantly, "An acreage to the north of town. He's already bought it and is in the process of transferring it to Verna's name. He's looked at buying some other properties and submitted some well-thought-out plans to turn them to rental properties. Doesn't mean he's not using it as a front to launder money, though."

"And if that's the case, then I'll help you bring him down," Peter promised. "The fact is, I don't believe Marconi had anything to do with Frankie's death."

"I hate it, but I think you're right." Donnelly pulled a folder from a drawer and tossed it to Peter. "I got that from the FBI. They've been keeping tabs on Marconi, too. Seems as though he hasn't visited Pine Grove in a few months. The night before Frankie's death, he was in New York of all places. He couldn't have opened up the cabinet to let the spores out."

Peter's shoulders slumped in relief. Even though he was fairly certain he was on the right track with all of this, there was still that little voice in the back of his head that wondered if he was getting played for a sucker.

"That begs the question as to why Marconi told me he had no alibi for the time of Frankie's death," he muttered.

"My guess is that he was doing something even worse," Donnelly said darkly.

That was a good point. Though Marconi was a good nephew to Verna, he was still in the mob. You didn't just leave it. This whole land grab thing seemed suspicious, but it wasn't connected to Frankie Isles. Right now, they needed to concentrate on the case at hand. Then, afterward, they could focus on getting the mob out of Pine Grove. For good this time.

"Captain, I'm not going to lie. I have a great fondness for Verna, and my relationship with Marconi is more friendly than I'd like." Peter paused, then shook his head, sighing. "He was friends with my dad and has looked out for me in the past. Even helped me get the evidence I needed for some cases. That doesn't mean I want to be involved in his... activities."

Donnelly tapped his fingers against the top of his desk. "Then we'll have to put something together, Myer. For now, this isn't enough evidence that Henry Clay killed Frankie Isles. We have motive, sure, and knowledge, but that isn't enough to convince a jury."

"I know." Peter folded his arms, a wry smile crossing his face.

It was ironic that after years of Donnelly being aggressive and hostile toward him, they were working so well together. Peter hadn't ever thought he'd make a good cop. He was a lawyer and he was happy with that. Things had changed a great deal since he retired and moved to Pine Grove. He had thought he'd end up bored with nothing to do... but he'd found plenty to do in the years since.

Donnelly leaned forward, his chair creaking under the shift of weight. His eyes held a rare glint of trust, tempered by his usual skepticism. A frown was heavy on his face but there was an eagerness to the way he held himself, too.

"I'll admit, you've done more than I thought you would, Myer. Maybe you're not bringing in Marconi on this case, but I have to admire a man that sticks with it, even when he suspects someone he'd rather not be involved. We need more physical evidence, though. You think there's something in the attempted break-in six months ago we can use?"

"You mean like paint chips on Henry's tools?" Peter suggested.

Donnelly nodded once. "I'll get a warrant to check out his tools. Doubt we'll find anything, but it just might be enough to spook him, make him slip up."

Sam moved around the desk and lifted a paw to Donnelly to shake, his tail wagging. Donnelly stared at Sam and inched back.

"Get your dog under control," he snapped.

"Sam," Peter called, tugging his leash gently. He was surprised at the captain's reaction to Sam, especially when Sam was being so quiet. He narrowed his eyes slightly. He hadn't realized that Donnelly was scared of dogs before now!

"I'm gonna get that warrant," Donnelly said, his face turning red. He jumped to his feet. "You'd best have a plan to catch Henry in action, Myer. Because that's the only way we're going to get him for this murder."

CHAPTER
TEN

THE GREENHOUSE, shadowed in moonlight, was filled with the heady aroma of various flowering plants. The heat of the day clung on, making sweat bead Peter's forehead as he crouched among the rows of plants. Captain Donnelly waited close by, in a different row so they had better chance of triangulating Henry if—when—he came. Donnelly had stripped out Henry's shed earlier in the day.

If he was going to make a move, it would be tonight.

There was no telling when Henry would arrive, though, so Peter adjusted his position to be more comfortable and closed his eyes to meditate. Thoughts of Jessica filled his mind. He'd introduced her to his kids earlier in the year. Rina and Matt both liked her. She'd even gotten along with Peter's ex-wife at Matt's wedding.

He felt as though he'd known Jessica forever. And how calm and reassuring she'd been with this business with Sam only solidified it. Peter smiled to himself. When he divorced Melanie, he never thought he'd fall in love again... and yet he had.

The greenhouse door creaked open. Peter moved stealthily, rolling to the balls of his feet. Using the plants as cover, he peered through their foliage. A figure shrouded in shadow crept along the far wall, toward the back wall. There, he turned on a flashlight, revealing his face. Henry Clay. So, they had their proof he could get into the greenhouse. But what was he doing?

Henry slowly made his way along the wall, scattering something behind him. From the sound of it hitting the ground, it sounded like sand. Kitty litter, maybe?

Peter's heart beat faster as he carefully made his way down the aisle he was in, making sure not to make any sound. His senses were on high alert, listening to the soft shuffling footsteps from Henry. The man was muttering to himself.

"We don't need no cat sanctuaries anyway. Crazy old woman. Best to just get her out of town. I didn't do anything anyone else wouldn't if they were in my shoes." His voice came out a harsh whisper, as though he was trying to convince himself.

Peter made it to the end of the aisle. Henry put the flashlight on a table and pulled on a pair of latex gloves. To Peter's surprise, Henry then pulled a second pair of latex gloves out of an envelope. A strange scent wafted into the air, then Peter suddenly identified it—it smelled like Verna's house.

Henry opened the cabinet and put the second latex gloves into the corner and shut it again. He carefully tore the tip of the finger out, leaving it pinched in the cabinet. And Peter knew exactly what he was doing. Verna used that type of glove when she changed her cat litter. Henry had stolen the gloves and was planting it here, hoping to frame Verna.

"That should seal it," Henry muttered. His shoulders sagged as he snapped off his own gloves.

Peter straightened from his hiding place. "Seal what exactly, Henry?"

Henry let out a shriek, grabbing his flashlight. He shone it in Peter's face. He shielded his eyes and stepped from the aisle.

"Peter Myer," Henry said, sounding nervous. "I was just... just seeing if I could take care of Frankie's flowers. She loved them so much, I'd hate for them to end up dead."

"Is that why you have access to the greenhouse? You know the code because she told it to you, so you could come in and look after her plants?" Peter asked.

Henry swallowed hard. "We might have hated each other, but I wouldn't let the plants suffer for it."

Peter decided to stop beating around the bush. He drew himself up and pointed at Henry. "No. You knew the code because you gave her the keypad, pretending to be friendly. You did your best to earn her trust by directing her ire on Verna. And now you're here to frame her, trying to get us to arrest her."

"I didn't," Henry said pathetically.

"You did. You knew how to poison her. That's why you put the ground-up poisonous plants with her homemade tea. You knew what to give her and in what amounts to start weakening her system. You knew about the plants in that cabinet. You found out about them last year when you weren't part of the Garden Club competition."

And that did it. Henry howled. "I wasn't part of the competition because she killed my beautiful hydrangeas! She killed them and nobody did anything. Even town hall was in her pocket! They moved the property lines to give her the right. She had no right! All I did was avenge my poor hydrangeas. She deserved it. She deserved all of it!"

He lunged for Peter but before he could get to him, Donnelly was there. Henry yelped as Donnelly tripped him, then lay sobbing into the ground as Donnelly put the cuffs on him.

"What's going to happen to my roses?" Henry cried as Donnelly pulled him to his feet. "My poor garden…"

"So, he really did it over the plants?" Jessica asked once Peter summed up the case.

Peter pet Sam absently, his gaze unfocused. "He loved his garden. I think it was a combination of things, years of strife. The hydrangeas were just the straw that broke the camel's back."

"And Marconi wasn't involved in the end," Jessica said.

"Not this time." Peter shook his head. Marconi was up to something, he was sure of it, but he didn't want to dwell on that right now. Instead, he put an arm around Jessica's shoulder and kissed her temple. "With the case over, I was thinking we could get out of town for a bit. Maybe go up the lake for some fishing."

Jessica nodded. "That sounds wonderful. It's been slammed lately, but I'm getting a new vet on staff so I should be able to relax a bit."

"Good." Peter enjoyed the feeling of her leaning into his side. "I love you, Jessica."

Jessica kissed him. "And I love you, Peter Myer."

The End

MAY DAY MURDER

A COZY MYSTERY

PROLOGUE

PINE GROVE, a pretty little town in New England, was all revved up for the May Day festival. Flowers were wrapped around all the streetlights and the storefronts had been decorated with motifs of various flowers. It was the most effort the town had ever put into the festival, which normally was little more than a sad picnic in Centennial Park with some boiled hot dogs and bored parents watching their kids run around.

This year was going to be different. Eleanor Hadley, planner extraordinaire, made sure of that. Eleanor nodded at the large maypole that had been set up, ready for the dance. She had gotten the local dance club to practice for months now, wanting a perfectly synchronized movement to wow everyone.

"It looks wonderful, Eleanor," her assistant, Lisa, said.

"Of course it does. You don't think I would do anything that isn't wonderful, do you?" Eleanor asked sharply.

Lisa flinched. She was a decent enough assistant, at least in a place like this. Eleanor had thought retiring to a little town such as Pine Grove would be a charming place to live out her years. What she found was... lackluster, if she was honest. She had worked hard all her life, and now all she had to look forward to was a weekly art meetup.

So, when she was given the chance to head up the May Day celebrations, she jumped at the chance.

Lisa shuffled off. Eleanor ignored her. A buzzing came from her pocket and she pulled out her phone. It was an email. Text message. Whatever.

Eleanor poked her tongue between her teeth as she jabbed her finger into the screen. A message popped up from a familiar number. *It's real,* the message read.

Triumph washed through her and she shoved her phone back into her pocket. At last! Finally, she was going to be vindicated. She'd show them. She'd show them all!

CHAPTER
ONE

PETER MYER'S Monday morning strolls with Jessica and the dogs had become his favorite part of the week. While they spent lots of time together, there was something rejuvenating about this particular time. With his labrador, Sam, and her beagle, Charlie, they always had a leisurely stroll through the woods near the Myer residence, enjoying how full of life nature was.

This morning, it was interrupted by Captain Richard Donnelly, who called him to Centennial Park.

"And you might as well bring Dr. Stern with you," Donnelly grumbled. "There's been a murder. Eleanor Hadley was found this morning wrapped up in the ribbons around the maypole, strangled to death."

"Jessica's with me," Peter said, giving Jessica a quick glance. She nodded and Peter added, "We'll be there in ten minutes."

Soon enough, the two of them were on the scene. Sam and Charlie trotted next to them, relaxed on their leashes. As they approached Donnelly and the maypole, Peter and Jessica tied the leashes to a nearby fencepost. The two dogs stretched out on the ground, heads on their paws as they waited patiently. It didn't stop Donnelly from casting them a suspicious look—he didn't like dogs.

"Myer," Donnelly greeted with a little less than his usual tacit dislike. "Glad you got here so fast. You're going to have to take lead on this case."

Peter's eyebrows lifted toward his hairline. "You feeling okay, Captain?"

"Don't get smart with me. I have a very busy workload right now and you'll only stick your nose in it anyway," Donnelly snapped. He waved two folder files at him. "I've got the paperwork here for you and Dr. Stern to become official consultants, temporary officers, whatever you want to call it."

"Thank you, Captain," Jessica said, surprised. "I guess this helps with lawyers trying to get the murderers free by claiming we didn't follow due process."

Donnelly shoved the folders into Peter's hands. "We're just lucky that Myer here was able to argue out of it, especially since you somehow managed to always get confessions. Now. I'm sure that you know what to do. I really have to get back to that big case I'm working on."

Peter nodded. "Thanks. We'll get this filled out and back to you by the end of the day."

He knew better than to ask what case Donnelly was working on, though he was curious. Better not poke the bear. Donnelly hesitated a moment longer before blowing out a huffed breath and stalking off. Peter and Jessica shared amused glances before they focused on the crime scene. Peter was glad to see that it wasn't particularly gruesome. In fact, Eleanor seemed almost as though she was sleeping.

"She wasn't strangled by the ribbons, though it looks like the killer tried to set the scene as though she did," Donnelly said. "We found rope fibers on her body. It's a black rope, which isn't a color you normally see."

"Who found the body?" Jessica asked a uniformed officer who was processing the scene.

"Leah Peabody," he answered.

Peter repressed a grimace. Back when he was going to high school here in Pine Grove, Leah was the queen bee and head 'mean girl.' The years hadn't been kind to her since, though she retained that bitter tongue of hers. He and Jessica headed over to where she was, leaning against the public restrooms. An unlit cigarette was clutched between her fingers as she stared at it.

As they approached, Peter was surprised at the difference he saw since he's last interacted with Leah. Then, she'd been wearing worn clothes with stained fingertips and a dull look in her eyes. Her clothes were still fairly old, but fit her better. Despite holding the cigarette, there was no smell of smoke around her. Her eyes were brighter, too, and her hair looked glossier.

She frowned at the two of them as they approached and dropped the unlit cigarette into the trash. "Trying to give it up," she muttered. "But finding a dead body makes you reconsider."

"You look great," Jessica said.

Leah offered her a small smile. "My doctor put me on multivitamins. Apparently, I wasn't having my nutritional needs met. Took me off my diet, too. But I guess I feel better," she admitted.

Jessica nodded. "Yeah, it's easy to enter into that malnourished mode if you're not careful. I'm glad that you're doing better. You were part of the May Day planning team this year, right?"

"Yup."

"What can you tell us about Eleanor?"

Leah wrinkled her nose. "Eleanor was... passionate. She had a vision and wanted to make sure that everything fit within that vision. She was difficult to get along with and very domineering. I didn't like her, and we didn't get along. But even I can admit that she was doing an amazing job here. It was going to be something that nobody in this town had ever seen before."

As she finished talking, Leah's shoulders slumped. Despite her harsh words about Eleanor, there was a trace of true sadness in her words. Peter made a mental note of it. He and Jessica then went to inspect the scene as Eleanor's body was taken away. There were no footprints in the area, but one of the forensic team found a piece of torn paper near the maypole.

"This doesn't feel like normal paper," Jessica said as she smoothed it between her fingers. "Looks old."

Leah craned her neck to get a better look at it. "Eleanor was convinced that the Pine Grove treasure was real. That looks like a paper from the journal she was always carrying around."

Peter turned to Leah, his brows furrowed together. "Pine Grove treasure? You mean that old myth about the founding families burying all their valuables to hide them from the British?"

"That's the one," Leah said.

Charlie let out a yip, sitting up now. As Jessica and Peter went over to the dogs, Peter tucked the paper into an evidence bag. He'd have it analyzed. But one thing was clear—he had a feeling that this murder was more than just a grudge against an over-eager party planner.

He'd never believed in the treasure. Not really. Was he about to be proved wrong?

CHAPTER
TWO

AFTER PROCESSING THE SCENE, Peter called the number of Lisa Jon-Smith, Eleanor's assistant. Leah recalled seeing Eleanor screaming at poor Lisa for hours a few days ago. It wouldn't be the first time an abused assistant had gone off the deep end. Lisa agreed to let Peter and Jessica talk with her in the afternoon. The two took the opportunity to go to their favorite café and fill out the paperwork Donnelly had given them.

"Odd change of heart for Donnelly, isn't it?" Jessica mused.

Peter nodded. "I suppose he has his reasons. I'm just glad that we're going about it all officially this time."

Jessica laughed. Peter grinned. He loved the sound of her laughter. It lit up every room they were in, always bright and cheerful. He loved the way she tossed her hair as she laughed, the way her eyes sparkled. There wasn't anything about her that he didn't love. His heart started to beat faster as the words he'd been thinking more and more pressed against his lips. But now wasn't the right time—he had to wait, to be patient.

Soon, they were at Lisa's house. She was a tiny, frail-looking young woman. Peter would have guessed she was in her early teens if not for what he knew about her. One thing was clear, though. A person as small and thin as Lisa wouldn't have the strength to strangle someone of Eleanor's height and weight.

That didn't mean they wouldn't get information from her, though.

"You can bring the puppies inside," Lisa said, smiling at Sam and Charlie.

"Thank you," Peter said, leading Sam in.

Lisa led them to the living room.

"Eleanor wanted everything to be perfect," Lisa said as she sat on her sofa, wringing her hands. Charlie, his tail wagging in wide, friendly sweeps, went over to her and put his head in her lap. "I took her position as assistant because I'd followed her career before she retired. But she was more than a perfectionist. She was a tyrant. She screamed at me for everything and changed her mind on a dime, then pretended like she hadn't."

"That must have been difficult to take," Peter said sympathetically.

Lisa nodded. "I decided to quit after the May Day celebration. It was so close, I thought I could hang on long enough to see it through. I wouldn't have hurt Eleanor. Even if she was awful, I'm not that sort of person."

Peter nodded, keeping his expression blank so as not to give anything away. "Can you think of anyone else that she had trouble with?"

"Tom Merriweather," Lisa answered. She absently pet Charlie's silky ears. "The town historian. I saw them arguing in her office the other day and they clammed up as soon as they realized I was there. They were saying something about a map, I think."

Jessica leaned forward. "A map to the Pine Grove treasure, perhaps?"

To Peter's surprise, Lisa snorted. "That was the one thing I didn't understand. Why was she so obsessed with that legend? I grew up in Pine Grove and she drilled me about it endlessly. She's not even from here. But she didn't seem to understand the endless treasure-hunting that has gone around this place."

Peter chuckled despite himself. Sam lifted his head and thumped his tail against the ground, giving him a doggy smile. "Is it still a rite of passage to bring back a lump of coal from that abandoned mine and claim it's the treasure?"

Lisa laughed as she nodded. "It is! Captain Donnelly kept trying different ways to block out the kids, but finally reinforced the entrance to the mine and dumped a bunch of coal throughout the space and sealed off the back of it."

"Did he?" Jessica asked, surprised.

"I guess he figured that it was the best way to keep kids safe, since they were constantly finding their way in there anyway," Lisa answered. "Though maybe it wasn't enough. Eleanor claimed she found this antique key in the mines, but if it was in the main chamber, it would have been found ages ago."

Jessica shared a puzzled look with Peter and asked, "A key?"

Lisa nodded. "She kept it on her person at all times. The one time I saw it on her desk, she'd told me to tidy up. I didn't even touch it and she came barging in, screaming at me not to touch it. She made me turn out my pockets, accusing me of making a mold of it."

"That doesn't seem like very stable behavior," Peter observed. He rubbed the back of his neck as he considered this. "There wasn't a key found on her body. Could she have left it somewhere?"

"After the desk incident, she put it on a chain and wore it around her neck," Lisa answered. "I can't see her leaving it anywhere else."

Peter made a mental note to double-check. If the key wasn't found, then it might be a link to the killer. "Do you know why she was at the maypole this morning?"

Lisa shook her head. "She might have been attending to some last-minute details. I don't know. She was so fastidious. It could have been that she decided to change the color palette at the last minute. I don't know who she would have called to help her with that, though. I never got a message from her."

Peter and Jessica thanked Lisa and left the house. Back in the car, Jessica scratched Charlie's ears as she mused aloud, "So, we have two possible motives here. The May Day celebration and the Pine Grove treasure. Do you think this key is part of the case? Maybe the killer took it and that's why it wasn't on the body."

"Someone else might have taken Eleanor's confidence that she'd found a clue to the treasure seriously," Peter agreed.

"To the museum?" Jessica suggested, her eyes brightening.

"That's exactly what I was thinking."

Jessica grinned and clipped the dogs into their safety restraints before pulling on her own seatbelt. Peter admired the efficient way she worked. They were so in tune, and he was pleased that Donnelly had accepted that they'd be working on the case together. Thinking of Donnelly... what was he up to? There seemed to be something else going on, something Peter couldn't quite put his finger on.

He shook his head and started off. One case at a time. They had to solve Eleanor's murder, and then they'd look into the case of the police captain.

CHAPTER
THREE

THERE WAS a big sign on the doorway of the museum that read *Service animals only.* Peter and Jessica glanced at each other, and then at the two dogs they'd brought along. Sam and Charlie stared back at them, looking like angelic little creatures.

"I'll take them over to the dog park and let them run around," Jessica volunteered. "You know how to question people better than I do."

Peter laughed and kissed her. "Alright. I'll make sure to catch you up when it's done."

Jessica kissed him back, longer than the one he'd given her. "I'll hold you to it."

"Woof!" said Sam.

Charlie sat on his haunches and lifted his head as though he was going to bay, but Sam nudged him, nearly toppling him over. They started to mouth each other playfully instead. Peter laughed as Jessica detangled their leashes and pulled them away.

Peter stepped into the museum and was soon greeted by Tom. He was in every respect the sexy historian that would be found in a holiday romance movie. Tall, broad-shouldered, with wavy dark hair that was nonetheless conservative. He peered at Peter with undisguised suspicion as Peter came into the museum.

"Can I help you with anything?" he asked coolly.

"I'm Peter Myer. Captain Donnelly asked me to look into Eleanor Hadley's murder," Peter answered.

Tom folded his hands over his desk. "Is that so? What brings you here?"

"You were seen having an argument with the victim several days ago." Peter kept his voice flat. He didn't want this to end up in a hostile stand-off, though Tom seemed to be oddly on guard already.

"I... suppose we had a disagreement," Tom said stiffly. "She had this wild idea that she'd found a key that would unlock a secret underground vault containing ancient treasure."

Peter nodded. "The Pine Grove treasure. Legend has it that during the Revolutionary War, the founding families of Pine Grove were afraid that the British would loot their goods, and so created a vast space where they hid all their treasures. But the only man who knew where it was died during a cholera outbreak."

"Which is ridiculous," Tom said, shaking his head. "Why would all those families pool their most valued possessions and leave it in the hands of a single person? How would he have been able to stash everything with nobody else knowing where he was taking it? It's all nonsense. But she thought she found a map that showed the location of the vault."

Peter's mind flashed to the piece of paper they found at the scene. "A key and a map?"

"Yes," Tom said.

"And you disagreed with her on this?"

Tom folded his arms. "I thought perhaps it was linked to a certain research project I'm doing. The map could have showed me the original configuration of Pine Grove, but Eleanor refused to show it to me while insisting that I help her find the treasure. The only thing is..." He hesitated before he pulled open a desk drawer. "Eleanor stopped in here yesterday and gave me this."

He handed over a thick, leather-bound book. Peter flipped it open to find lines upon lines of what appeared to be utter gibberish.

"Did she tell you why she was giving it to you?" Peter asked, his brow furrowed.

Tom shrugged. "She said that she thought someone had broken into her house. I told her to call the police, but she said Donnelly was 'in on it,' whatever that means. Honestly, I'm not sure she was all there, if you know what I mean." He tapped his temple.

Peter pocketed the journal, nodding his thanks. It might not seem like much, but it was something… if he could figure out what it meant. And if it meant anything at all, or if Eleanor was just pulling a prank on Tom.

"IT LOOKS LIKE A CIPHER TO ME," Jessica said, peering at the pages of the journal. "Look at this. The patterns are all very similar and follows what you'd expect in the structure of English grammar. My guess is that it's a simple replacement cipher, the kind that you see in the newspaper. I bet I can figure it out."

She dug into her purse for the notebook she always carried with her. Quickly, she found all the instances of a single letter on the page and made a list of them. These would be 'a' or 'I.' The three-letter words were a bit trickier. There were several repeating ones in the middle of sentences. These were likely 'and' or 'was,' while the three-letter words that often were at the start of sentences was more likely to be 'the.'

Peter leaned in closer, watching her work. "You're really good at this."

"I play a lot of this sort of word game," Jessica said. "Every morning in bed before I get up."

"That's good to know," Peter said, nodding.

Something about the way he said it made her heart jump. He said it like he was planning on seeing her ritual for himself. She was distracted from the cipher, studying his profile. At her intensity, Peter gave her a quizzical look.

Jessica shook herself. "Um, I also learned that Eleanor had bought the old Walker barn. She's been trying to get Ben Harper to do something with it."

"Where did you hear about that?" Peter asked, looking impressed.

"Mr. Forth was here with his pug," Jessica answered, gesturing at the dog park. Sam and Charlie were chasing each other nearby, though they were careful to stay close to their people. "He was complaining about the contracting company not getting his kitchen done as quickly as he wanted."

Peter rubbed his chin. "Lisa didn't say anything about that."

Jessica nodded. "To be fair, it doesn't have anything to do with the May Day celebrations. But when I asked Mr. Forth about the Pine Grove treasure, he said that barn was supposed to hold a clue as to its location. But he followed up by saying the original burned in the fifties, so it's unlikely to still have anything."

"It's a good next step, anyway. Come here, Sam," Peter called. "We're going to go see a contractor."

CHAPTER
FOUR

"HEY THERE," Ben said as he entered the office. "I heard you were looking for me."

Peter and Jessica had come to the contractor's office nearly half an hour ago. The secretary, a round-faced woman with greying hair, had called Ben and told them he had visitors. She then assured them he'd be right in. She'd promptly ignored them and the ringing telephone to love on Sam, who lapped up the attention as though he'd never been pet before.

"I'm Peter Myer and this is Dr. Jessica Stern," Peter said, shaking Ben's hand.

Ben nodded. "Dr. Stern, right. We met last year when I brought in a couple abandoned kittens I found on a project. Turns out they weren't abandoned. And they were bobcats. Their mama was not happy." He laughed, but there was a strange edge to it, as though he was talking too much and he knew it. "Right. So, what's this about anyway?"

"Eleanor Hadley."

Ben grimaced. "I heard about her. Not going to lie, I can't say I'm surprised that someone took her out. She wanted me to dismantle this old barn piece by piece but not damage anything. And for the price I quoted for out-and-out demolition, too!"

Jessica winced. "That sounds like quite the bait-and-switch she pulled."

"Yeah. Luckily, nothing had been signed and no money exchanged hands." Ben shrugged. "All I had to do was cut her loose. Was going to give her one more chance to be reasonable. Guess that's not something I have to worry about anymore."

"Do you know why she was so interested in that barn?" Peter asked. Before Ben could answer, though, Peter's phone started ringing. It was Donnelly. "Sorry, I have to take this." He answered and held the phone to his ear. Before he could get out a single word, Donnelly barked, "Get to the station. I have a lead for you."

PETER'S MOUTH was drawn into a thin line as he stood across the desk from Donnelly. Jessica didn't blame his rising temper, though someone like Donnelly wouldn't see that Peter was upset. He was the most even-tempered person Jessica knew. Sam and Charlie sat next to Peter's feet, looking up at him as though they sensed the tension in him.

"Eleanor had a cousin in Pine Grove?" Peter repeated.

Donnelly nodded. "Lisa what's-her-name just called it in. Apparently, they were estranged and there was some sort of dispute over inheritance."

"You could have told me this over the phone," Peter said, nettled.

Jessica stepped forward. She didn't want this to devolve into an argument, which was where it seemed to be heading. She cleared her throat and caught Donnelly's attention. As she did so, she slid her hand into Peter's and squeezed lightly. Some of the tension eased from his jawline.

"We have quite a bit of evidence that points to Eleanor being interested in the Pine Grove treasure," she said. "What do you know about the legend?"

Donnelly's eyebrows lifted toward his hairline. "Eleanor was interested in the treasure?"

"That's right. She seemed to think she had a map," Peter said. "And she wanted a contractor to take apart an old barn, presumably to look for clues."

Donnelly leaned back in his chair. "Huh. Funny. I thought an elegant city woman like that would be too smart to believe in the legend. Locals, I get. They grow up with the romance of the treasure and are so bored in life what else are they going to do? But her? Huh. Maybe her cousin will know. Margaret Hadley—Pine Grove born and bred. Go talk to her, Myer. Maybe there's something you'll learn."

PETER ROLLED his shoulders as he stepped out of the car. The day was cool and cloudy, so he went to the door first while Jessica rolled down the windows for the dogs. This early in the year there wasn't much danger of overheating, especially with the scent of rain in the air, but one couldn't be too careful. She sat in the car with them as Peter knocked on the door.

Soon, a woman with a stern look and strong jaw answered the door. "Yes?"

Peter introduced himself and what they were here for. Margaret's expression softened and she invited him to sit on the porch with her. Jessica joined them.

"Eleanor wasn't easy to get along with," Margaret said when Peter explained the circumstances. "She claimed a bunch of property around here as part of her inheritance after our grandparents died. The will clearly stated it was meant to go to me, but she took it to court. I didn't have the money to fight her."

"So, she fleeced you?" Jessica asked, her brows pinched together.

Margaret shrugged. "You could say that. In the end, she offered me half of what the property was worth if I'd back out. I took it. She kept saying that she had such a special connection with the property because of the childhood days she and I spent here. I didn't believe it… I bet she thought it had something to do with the treasure."

"You don't believe in it?" Peter asked.

Margaret shook her head. "Not at all. But Eleanor did, ever since we were girls. She was convinced that she had found a piece of it when we were young and snuck into that old mineshaft. I always thought she got somebody's lost coin."

Jessica dug out Eleanor's journal and her notebook. "We have Eleanor's journal, but it's written in some sort of cipher. I've started figuring it out, but hoped you could help."

"Of course, dear." Margaret took the two books and gazed at them. "Oh, this is the same cipher we used as children. We passed notes during Sunday services. Let me just..." She wrote down a few things in Jessica's notebook. Peter leaned forward, trying to see. "There you are. That should be enough for you to figure it out."

Peter grinned as Margaret passed Jessica back the book. "Thank you, Miss Hadley. You've been more helpful than you know."

CHAPTER
FIVE

THE BARN that Eleanor wanted to take apart was weathered and gray, leaning slightly to one side. Its metal roof was rusted and there was moss growing on the north side of the building. All in all, not much worth saving. Peter was a little anxious as he and Jessica made their way inside. The barn certainly didn't seem stable. He was glad that they had elected the leave the dogs at Jessica's apartment while they came to inspect the building.

Inside smelled of dust and hay, much like any other barn. While the structure still didn't seem to be very stable, it wasn't as bad from the inside as it was from the outside. An old John Deere tractor, the kind with a closed-in cab, sat in the middle of the barn. Its green paint was scratched and when Peter peered inside, the seat was covered in dust and the cushion torn. The keys were in the ignition and judging by the faint smell of gasoline, someone had filled it up recently.

"I'm not sure what we're going to find here," Jessica said slowly as she walked in a circle around the tractor. "Eleanor wanted to take it apart, so there won't be any clues just laying out in the open."

"Maybe not, but it's a lovely spot for a date, don't you think?" Peter asked jokingly.

Jessica answered with one of her sunny laughs. His heart skipped a beat. It seemed like the more time they spent together, the more her presence affected him. He loved it.

"Speaking of dates, do you want to catch a movie on Friday? It's a kid's movie playing at the Pine Grove theatre, but we could go up to the city for more options," she suggested.

"Sounds good." Peter smiled at her. "You know, I really love how my life has settled here in Pine Grove. And I love you. I'm glad that we took that step to actually talk about our relationship."

Jessica nodded her agreement. They'd spent too long dancing around whether they were a couple or not. Even after their first kiss. Luckily, once they'd discussed their relationship, they found they were on the same page. Peter hesitated. If he asked his question now, would she be caught off guard? Or did she feel the pull towards the same place as he did?

"You know, Rina and Matt have both been messaging me," Jessica said. "I'm supposed to let you know that you need to come to the cabin when they invite you, because they're planning a surprise party for you."

Peter frowned. "But isn't a surprise party meant to be a surprise?"

"I asked Rina about that," Jessica answered with a shrug. "She said the surprise would be that you know and still have to act surprised."

Peter chuckled as he shook his head. His daughter could be a little eccentric at times. It was a good thing, though. After he divorced Melanie, Rina's normally exuberant personality had tempered for a few years. Now that she was back to herself, it was a relief. It showed that she was healing from the situation, too.

Peter rounded the tractor and slid his arms around Jessica's waist from behind. She leaned into him and they shared a kiss. Even in this creepy barn, a feeling of excitement and comfort washed through Peter. There was nobody on this world he'd rather be with than Jessica.

"I think you're right," he said after they broke apart. "There aren't going to be any clues here. If there was anything, Eleanor would have found it. I think we're barking up the wrong tree—the legend is a distraction. We need to focus on who had a motive to kill her."

"Aren't we operating under the thought that the legend is the motivation?" Jessica asked, arching one of her brows. They headed for the barn doors.

Peter hummed in thought. "I don't see how anyone would believe it enough to kill her over it, especially since we have no proof she found anything."

He reached to open the door, but it didn't move. Frowning, he started to yank, then push against it. Still nothing. What had happened? Jessica gasped.

"Peter, look!" she pointed. Curls of grey smoke had started to seep under the door and through the open slats in the side of the barn.

Peter's heart jumped to his throat. In an instant, he knew what was happening. Someone had locked them into this barn and set it on fire! His blood rushed through his ears as he looked back, searching for something that would help them break open the door. The dry, dusty air would help the fire spread quickly as soon as it was inside… Luckily, the outside was still damp from the rain. But the smell of gasoline must mean that someone had used it…

Only the smoke was grey. Gasoline smoke was black. Which meant there wasn't an accelerant at all. So, what was the smell?

"The tractor," he cried.

Jessica grabbed his hand and they raced for it. Peter helped Jessica inside first and climbed in after her. She was already in the seat, turning over the engine as he shut the door behind them. The smoke curled around the glass windows but the seals on the cab held. The engine roared to life and Jessica shoved it into gear, then hurtled toward the doors.

Peter braced himself for the impact. The tractor barely jolted as they slammed into the flimsy doors, sending them crashing to either side behind them. As the tractor bounced over the uneven ground, Peter looked back. Large piles of brush had been built up around the barn. This was no accident…

"You're right," he said grimly. "There's more to the legend than I realized. Someone is willing to kill for it."

CHAPTER
SIX

AFTER REPORTING to Donnelly and taking a long, hot shower, Jessica was ready to collapse into bed. It had gotten dark outside some time ago. Normally she didn't mind nighttime, and even enjoyed sitting on her balcony with a cup of herbal tea. Today, though, she kept the curtains shut to lock out the night and any prying eyes that it might hide.

"It might not have been a great attempt at killing us, but it was still an attempt," she told Charlie as he hopped up onto the sofa next to her.

Charlie licked her cheek and settled into the cushion with a sigh.

Jessica sighed, stroking his silky ears. Even with the day's scare, she didn't want to stop investigating with Peter. She loved solving cases with him. It was strange, how quickly she'd grown accustomed to helping him out in these things. For most of her life, she didn't think it was something she'd want to do. She loved being a veterinarian, even with its challenges.

"Peter just opened up my world," she told Charlie as she picked up Eleanor's journal. "And I fall a little more in love with him every day."

Charlie wagged his tail and closed his eyes.

With a laugh, Jessica settled deeper into the sofa. She opened Eleanor's journal and went back to translating it. Peter had offered to stay with her, or to have her come to his place after their scare. But Jessica wasn't so easily frightened; besides, the sofa wasn't very comfortable to sleep on and she didn't want to put Peter through waking up with a bad back.

"Let's see if I can find our next clue, eh?" she said as she painstakingly started to translate each word.

"SHE SAYS that something is buried near the oak," Jessica said, showing Peter the page she'd translated last night. They were back in Centennial Park, near the only oak tree in the park.

Sam and Charlie were both secured to a nearby picnic table as the two detectives studied the big tree.

"How near it, though?" Peter wondered aloud.

As they started to circle the oak tree, Charlie let out a single, startled bark. Jessica turned, expecting a squirrel or some such thing. Instead, she found Tom Merriweather standing not ten feet away. He jumped and looked guilty when she stared at him in surprise. Next to her, Peter straightened and frowned.

"Have you seen a cat?" Tom asked quickly.

Jessica frowned as she glanced around. "No. What does it look like?"

"It's black and white," Tom said. "With white paws. If you find him, he answers to the name of Chester."

"We'll let you know if we see him," Peter said.

Tom hesitated then hurried off, glancing over his shoulder at them nervously. Jessica and Peter shared a puzzled look. That was strange. Charlie and Sam remained standing on their feet, apparently sensing the shift in the energy.

Peter shook his head. "That was weird."

"Yeah." Jessica pointed to a spot near the roots of the oak. "Look, there's some fresh-turned dirt here."

She brushed some of the dirt aside and gasped. The glint of metal shone from beneath the dirt. Bending, Jessica snatched it up. It was an old key, made from bronze that had tarnished to a greenish color. She rubbed the dirt off on her thigh and help it up. A broken chain hung from the one end.

"You think this was the key Eleanor kept with her?" she asked Peter.

Peter took it, inspecting the key. "I'd bet it was."

"But why is it here?" Jessica wondered.

Peter pocketed the key. "My guess is that Eleanor realized she was being followed. She wanted to keep the key from being taken, so she buried it here. My guess is the killer found her right after she hid it. But not soon enough to see where she'd hid it. When Eleanor refused to hand it over, the killer killed her."

"And then searched her body for the key, but was unable to find it," Jessica breathed.

"That looks like what's happened."

Jessica shook her head slowly, her heart aching. That was awful! She couldn't imagine what those final moments would have been. Did Eleanor wish she'd given up the key? What could be so important it was worth dying—and killing—for? Even if this Pine Grove treasure was real, was it really that valuable?

"I think there's something else in here," Peter said, bending. He pulled a glove onto his hand and scooped out handfuls of earth. It came out easily, clearly having been loosened earlier. About a foot down, he reached a lockbox.

Excitement flared through Jessica. She dropped to her knees and pulled it out, accidently shouldering Peter out of the way as she did so.

"Oops, sorry," she said sheepishly.

Peter only laughed and held a hand out to her. She passed him the lockbox then got to her feet and brushed off her pants. They went to the picnic table where the dogs were and set the box down. It was old, in that same bronzy metal that the key was. Peter pulled the key back out and tried it. It fit perfectly.

Holding her breath, Jessica flung open the chest. Inside was... "Paper?" she asked in surprise.

Peter lifted the top one out. It was old, crinkled and faded. The page cracked at the edge where Peter touched it and he quickly put it back.

"This is a census record from 1775," Peter said. "These are historical documents."

"And how much you want to bet that there's clues to the treasure in them?" Jessica crowed, her eyes bright.

Peter laughed. "You've been bit by the bug."

"Apparently. And I think I know exactly who can help us decipher this," Jessica said. She looked around to find Tom standing beneath an elm, looking up at a small dark shape in the branches—his missing cat, no doubt. "Our local historian is just the man."

CHAPTER
SEVEN

ON THE WAY to the museum, Jessica got a call from Lisa. "I think I might have something that you need to know. Can you meet me at Margaret Hadley's house?" Lisa asked, her voice shaking. From tears or something else?

"Of course," Jessica agreed. "I'll be right there."

Peter frowned at her as she hung up her phone. Jessica shook her head. "We can't bring the dogs into the museum, anyway."

Ahead of them, Tom pulled up next to the museum. He hopped out of his car and dashed in, all excited. It was, apparently, not his cat that he'd been looking for—and a giant squirrel he'd found. As soon as Peter and Jessica asked him about the documents they'd found, he had eagerly invited them to the museum to take a closer look at them.

Peter nodded once, sighing. "Be careful, Jess. We still don't know who tried to lock us in that barn."

Jessica parked the car, then kissed him. "You be careful, too."

Soon, she was at Margaret Hadley's house. Lisa and Margaret were inside already, but Margaret insisted they sit in the backyard since Jessica had the dogs with her. Sam put his head on Lisa's knee and gazed contentedly at her as she pet his head. Charlie, on the other hand, wandered around the yard sniffing everything.

"I heard Eleanor on the phone with someone the day before she died," Lisa said, looking unsettled. "I thought it was Margaret since Eleanor kept talking about 'our' family land. But when I finally worked up the courage to call the number, it was a man who answered. I don't know who it was, so I came here right away to ask Margaret if there was any other Hadleys in Pine Grove."

Jessica's brow furrowed. What? "I'm afraid I don't understand."

Margaret reached over to pat Lisa's hand. "The family property was under option a few years back to become a ski resort. The town shut it down, but there are thousands of acres of forest that have come back to me now. If there is another Hadley descendant in town, they might have a claim on the property, too."

The census records. Jessica's eyes widened. "Oh, my..."

"I think, from what I overheard, that Eleanor did find someone else who was a Hadley descendant," Lisa explained. "What if the treasure Eleanor was after was really land all along? With so much property.... You could get millions from selling it, and even more from developing it into resorts and the like. Like the ski resort," she added. "It was shut down because of environmental concerns, but there's always more that can be done."

Jessica leaned back, her gaze unfocused. That made a lot of sense. When it came to the natural beauty around Pine Grove, there was no limit as to what could be done to make money. Campgrounds, guided tours, small retreats...

A treasure trove indeed. Maybe the legend was true... just not in the way they thought.

"THESE ARE VERY OLD DOCUMENTS," Tom said reverently. He wore white cotton gloves as he separated the contents of the lockbox. "Census records... wills... This is all very, very exciting."

Peter resisted the urge to reach over and help him. All the paper looked so delicate that he was afraid of it breaking if it touched it. He clasped his hands behind his back—a habit from childhood, when his mother would tell him to keep his hands behind his back to avoid touching things in the store. As Tom sorted out the pages, Peter looked over them.

"As exciting as it is, I don't understand why Eleanor would go through such lengths to keep it secret," he said doubtfully. "Did she think there was a hidden code leading to the Pine Grove treasure?"

In answer, Tom snorted. "Knowing her, I wouldn't doubt it. She wouldn't have understood a real treasure if it was staring her in the face."

Peter bent over the census records. The ink was still crisp on the page, but the writing was tight and cramped, making it difficult to read. "As far as history goes, I can see why this would be valuable. Look, I can see Myer in the census. I didn't think my family had been in Pine Grove that long."

"I told her," Tom said smugly. "There's nothing more valuable than knowledge and history. Look at this here. It's the will for William Hadley, Eleanor's direct ancestor. We know from the records there was some struggle over the inheritance, namely around an illegitimate child he had. But Eleanor... knowing her, I bet she thought that she'd find instructions to some underground vault in this."

Peter leaned back and frowned at Tom. "She talked about it a lot with you, didn't she?"

Tom lifted his eyes. His face colored as he cleared his throat. "Well... I suppose she did."

"Who else did she talk to about it?" Peter pressed.

"Nobody," Tom said quickly.

Too quickly. He was hiding something. Peter narrowed his eyes and stepped a little closer, just close enough to make it uncomfortable. "Did you tell someone about it?"

Tom winced. He looked away and cleared his throat.

It was answer enough. Peter waited a little while longer, letting Tom think this through. Finally, he asked, "Who was it?"

"I... I don't think it means anything," Tom said guiltily.

"Who?" Peter repeated. His voice was flat.

Tom shuffled on the spot and bent his head. "A few days ago, I went to O'Hara's Pub. Ben joined me and bought me a beer... and another. He asked me all sorts of questions about Eleanor and that

barn. I don't know exactly how much I told him." He looked up miser-
ably, guilt haunting his gaze. "Is that why he killed her? Because I told
him about the treasure?"

"We don't know that Ben killed Eleanor," Peter answered, his mind
racing. It was true, they didn't know… but now, he had an idea of how
to find out.

CHAPTER
EIGHT

BEN'S SECRETARY once more told Peter that it'd 'only be a minute' before Ben arrived. Which was just as well for Peter. He nodded slightly to Jessica, who had both dogs with her. She led them over to the secretary and started to chat about the local shelter. The secretary eagerly latched onto the conversation, mentioning that she was looking to adopt a dog herself.

It gave Peter the perfect opportunity to slip out unnoticed. The construction site was noisy, with people working everywhere. Nobody paid him any attention as he sidled up to Ben Harper's truck. He pulled himself up on the tire and peered in.

A black rope sat coiled just under a tarp.

"Hey!" Ben came charging toward him. "What are you doing?"

Peter snapped on a pair of gloves and picked up the rope. "I've got a warrant," he answered as he hopped down. He carefully put the rope into an evidence bag as Ben came to a stop, panting. "Funny this, Eleanor Hadley was killed with a black rope. What do you want to bet that when I have this processed, we find her skin and DNA on it?"

Ben's eyes widened. His mouth opened and closed as the door to his office opened. Jessica came outside, her phone in her hand.

"You heard about the treasure," Peter said, keeping his voice even. "You told Eleanor you'd take apart her barn at half of what it should cost, in exchange for a cut of the treasure once you found it. When she refused, you tried to take the key by force."

Ben closed his eyes. "I don't know what happened. I lost control. She went running off, yelling she was going to call the police. I just... lost control. I went after her. I meant to reason with her. The next thing I knew, that rope was in my hands and..."

His shoulders slumped as Peter nodded at Jessica.

"Captain Donnelly," she said into the phone, "we have our killer."

"So, you killed Eleanor Hadley. And you tried to burn Jessica and me in that barn," Peter accused, his temper rising.

Ben's head jerked up. "No. No, that wasn't me. I wouldn't have burned the barn. It was the key. I needed the clues that were hidden. I wouldn't have hurt it."

"Turn around and put her hands on the truck," Peter said, disgusted. "You're under arrest."

He glanced over at Jessica, who gave him a small smile. It was over. Another case solved. Peter let out a sigh of relief. Time to put this behind him.

PETER STARED, aghast, at Donnelly. "What do you mean, Ben Harper was murdered last night?"

Donnelly rested his head in his hand, his elbow on his desk. "I came in this morning to find the officer I left on duty passed out. His coffee was laced with sedatives. Harper's dead. Stabbed in the chest."

"Why? He's the killer... who would want to kill him?" Peter asked, slumping into a chair.

"My guess? He wasn't acting alone," Donnelly answered. He lifted his head. There were dark circles ringing his eyes, making him look like he hadn't slept in a week.

Peter leaned forward, concerned. "The officer that was drugged. Is he okay?"

"Yeah. I'll have to look into him, of course, but I don't think he was involved. For all the things to happen in my own—" He cut off, looking over Peter's shoulder.

Peter turned. His eyes widened when he saw Marconi being led toward Donnelly's office. Marconi hesitated, narrowing his eyes when he saw Peter. Peter turned back to Donnelly, confusion sweeping through him.

"What does the mob have to do with the Pine Grove treasure and Eleanor Hadley's murder?" he asked aloud.

"It's unconnected to your case," Donnelly said, his voice tight.

Ah. So, this was the other case, the secret one, Donnelly was working on. The reason he'd handed Eleanor's murder off to Peter. It did little to assay Peter's confusion, but he bit down on the question he wanted to ask. Instead, he took his leave and went to take a look at the cells where Ben was killed. While he examined the scene, Jessica arrived.

Her face was pale. "I was trying to convince myself it wasn't true… How could this have happened?"

"I'm not sure." Peter ran his hands over his face. "But he was definitely killed by someone he knew. It has to be related to Eleanor's murder."

"Maybe Margaret? She stood to inherit all that property?" Jessica's question sounded doubtful to herself.

Peter dropped his hands. "Or it could be Lisa. If she knew more about the treasure than she told us, she could have arranged everything with Ben on the promise that she'd share what she found. And Tom… well, maybe he wasn't drunk when he told Ben about it."

"We have to review the evidence," Jessica said, her expression fierce and determined. "There's still a killer walking free… and we have to find out who it is."

CHAPTER
NINE

PETER SAT at an empty desk in the Pine Grove police department, studying over the evidence he had collected on the case. Who had motives in these murders? Eleanor had been verbally abusive to Lisa, but she claimed she was going to quit, which was a more reasonable answer to such abuses than murder was.

Then there was Margaret, who Eleanor had shuffled out of inheriting the vast properties around Pine Grove. She was given some value from the land, but not enough. Now she stood to inherit everything. Would she really go so far as to drug a cop and kill someone held in custody? If she was desperate enough, sure.

Tom Merriweather had been very excited about getting the documents Eleanor hid under the oak tree. He claimed it was for their historical value, but if anyone had enough pieces of the puzzle to find the Pine Grove treasure, it would be the town historian. Could someone who studied history really think that it was real, though?

The real question was how the officer on duty had been drugged and how the killer had managed to black out the cameras. Peter picked up the schematics for the security system here at the department. It was a detailed system with cameras covering all angles. Something about it tickled at the back of his mind and he squinted, then reached for the phone. There was another security system he wanted to see…

"WHAT CAN I GET FOR YOU?" Maeve, owner and bartender of O'Hara's Pub, asked Jessica with a toothy smile. She wore a brightly colored blue wig with various May flowers woven through the thick braids.

"Love your wig," Jessica said as she slid into a stool. "But nothing to drink today, Maeve. I'm here on official police business."

She had to bite back a giggle when saying that. Even though all the paperwork had been filled out, she still felt a bit like a kid playacting. Funny how she could have helped Peter with so many cases, but it was now that it started to feel surreal.

"So, it's information you're after." Maeve's eyes sparkled. "Alright, let's hear it."

"A few days ago, Tom Merriweather was here, yeah?" Jessica asked.

Maeve nodded. "He comes in every evening for supper. I know what night you're talking about, though. Normally he doesn't touch a drop of alcohol, but that night he ordered a few shots of whiskey. He started causing a scene, bragging about a big payday and complaining to everyone who would hear about Eleanor Hadley being too stubborn for her own good."

"Then what happened?"

"Ben Harper joined him and they left soon after. Funny thing, though," Maeve said, shaking her head. "When I cleaned up his table, the vase of flowers was full of liquid. Thought it was water at first, but it smelled an awful lot like whiskey. I guess he must have dropped a shot inside when he was getting too drunk."

Jessica smiled. "Or he didn't drink at all. Thank, Maeve. You've just cracked this case wide open."

Jessica and Peter met up just outside the museum and shared the information they had discovered. Armed with their combined knowledge, they marched into the museum. Tom was pouring over the census records they'd uncovered in Centennial Park. Peter glanced around, noting that the cameras here in the museum were from the same company that had installed the ones in the police department.

"What are you doing here?" Tom asked, startled.

Jessica put her hands on the desk and leaned forward, her normally kind face a mask of anger. "Tell me, Tom. Did you find the proof yet?"

"Proof?" Tom asked, looking at Peter. "What's she talking about."

"The reason why you convinced Ben Harper to kill Eleanor Hadley, and the reason you killed him," Peter said, folding his arms over his chest.

Tom sprang to his feet. "Me! I didn't kill anyone. Why would I kill them?"

Jessica tapped a finger against the census records. "This."

"Don't touch it, it's delicate," Tom cried, reaching to shove her hand away.

Peter narrowed his eyes and stepped closer menacingly. Tom swallowed and backed away. He quickly rounded the table and made shooing motions with his hands, like he was trying to drive them out of the museum.

"I don't know what you're talking about, but I won't have you poking and touching ancient documents. They're fragile and could easily be destroyed," he said, a thin sheen of sweat beading on his forehead.

"You found evidence that you were descended from the illegitimate daughter of William Hadley. Three hundred years ago, there was a challenge to William's will regarding how much she should inherit. And now, you thought if you could prove that you were her descendant, it would give you a claim to a portion of the property that the Hadleys own around town," Peter said, not budging.

Jessica nodded. "You used Eleanor's belief in the Pine Grove treasure to get her to find these documents, which were hidden during the Revolutionary War. But you must have tipped your hand, accidently let her know what was really going on. She told you she would bury you in lawsuits if you tried to touch her land."

Here, Peter picked up. "But you also knew Margaret. She's a much kinder person, and after being screwed over herself, she wouldn't want to do the same to someone else. With Eleanor out of the way, Margaret inherits and you would be able to manipulate her."

"I… didn't kill her," Tom said, shaking his head. "Ben Harper did!"

"Because you manipulated him, too," Peter said. "You told him you would get a huge payday if Eleanor died, and you'd hire him to develop the property. But once we figured out he killed Eleanor, you were afraid he'd tell us your part in it. So, you used the schematics of the museum security system to break into the police department's system. You delivered a coffee to the officer on duty and drugged him, then killed Ben."

Jessica sidestepped into Tom's path as he tried to skirt around them. "The barista identified your picture, Tom."

Tom looked between them and his shoulders slumped. "It wouldn't have happened if Eleanor wasn't so stubborn. If she wasn't so greedy. I just wanted what was mine. What should have been in my family for generations. It's those Hadleys... they've always been selfish. It's not my fault. She made me do it."

Peter and Jessica shared a grim look. Peter wondered if Tom really believed that. Either way... he pulled the handcuffs from his belt.

"Tom Merriweather, you are under arrest for the murder of Ben Harper," he said. As he cuffed the killer, he couldn't help but wonder if the Pine Grove treasure was more of a curse after all.

EPILOGUE

DONNELLY FROWNED as he turned off the recording of Tom Merriweather's confession. "How do you get them all to confess like that, Myer? I've never met so many killers so willing to spill their guts."

Peter couldn't help but laugh at Donnelly's disgruntled expression. "It's quite simple, Captain. You deal with hardened criminals. Every case I've solved was an amateur, someone who can't withstand the weight of questioning. So, of course they're going to be eager to relieve themselves of that burden."

"You might be right," Donnelly agreed, looking mollified. "Still, I can't argue with your results. That's another killer off our streets. I and the citizens of Pine Grove thank you, Peter. You have done a great service for us."

"Thank you, Captain," Peter said, shaking his hand.

Donnelly craned his neck. "So, where's Dr. Stern? I thought she'd want to be here to deliver the evidence, too."

"She had to get to the clinic. There was an emergency. She took the dogs with her," Peter added. "We know you don't like them."

"Now when have I ever said that?"

Peter ignored the disgruntled question and posed one of his own,

"Is your case with Marconi over, then? I saw him leaving the department when I was coming in."

Donnelly viewed him for a long moment before he nodded once, stiffly. "Yeah, you could say that. He and I have come to an agreement. He keeps the mob out of Pine Grove and doesn't do anything illegal, and I leave him and his aunt alone."

Surprise rippled through Peter. "It's all over that easily, is it?"

"Sometimes you have to do what's best for the town, even if it means making deals you'd rather not." Donnelly shrugged. "Marconi was using land sales to fund a money laundering scheme. I showed him what I knew and told him to stop it. Marconi might be mob, but he's one of the ones that you can trust to keep his word. Guess that's why he likes you so much," Donnelly added. "You're one of the good ones, Peter."

"Thank you, Captain," Peter said, oddly touched.

Donnelly's cheeks turned faintly pink. He grumbled under his breath. "Now get out of my office. I have work to do."

"Of course." Peter grinned as he left. It seemed like his relationship with the police captain had turned a corner.

THAT EVENING, Peter wrapped his arm around Jessica's shoulders as they watched the twilight descend over the forest. He'd spent so much of his life here in Pine Grove, but none of it was quite as peaceful as this moment. Despite the chill in the air, he felt warm and cozy with Jessica on one side and Sam on his other.

"I love my life," he murmured, smiling. "There was a time when I thought that it was impossible to be this happy."

Jessica rested her head on his shoulder. "I love my life, too. When I think about all the good we've done here in Pine Grove, I feel... very proud of myself. I never thought I'd get this sense of satisfaction from solving murders, but it's good. Solid. I feel like... like I'm building a solid foundation with you, Peter. All we have to do now is build a life together."

Peter kissed her temple. "That's how I feel, too."

As he gazed at her, a swell of emotion washed though him. He couldn't imagine his life without Jessica with him. The question he'd been waiting on sprang from his lips before he could stop it. "Will you marry me?"

Jessica's eyes widened, then a smile spread over her face. "Oh, Peter. I've been waiting for you to ask me. Yes. I will marry you." They kissed and Jessica giggled into his lips. "Life with you will never be boring, that's for sure."

Peter laughed in agreement. It really wouldn't be boring, that was certain. Pine Grove was still filled with plenty of mysteries to solve. He looked forward to figuring out what those mysteries were and resolving them one by one.

"Oh, I have something for you." Jessica fished into her pocket and held it out to him. "I saw it in a store the other day and I thought about you."

"What is it?" Peter asked, taking the delicate item.

Jessica watched his face as he studied it. It was a small mayflower keychain. It was made out of a smooth, polished wood and an inscription was written on the back of it. There was just enough light left in the day to make out the words.

"Every time we say the end, it's time for a new beginning," he read aloud.

"I thought it was a lovely sentiment," Jessica said, snuggling closer to him.

Peter pulled her closer, smiling. "I agree. It's the end of the case and the beginning of the rest of our lives. I love you, Jessica."

"I love you, too."

THE END

Did you enjoy *Pine Grove Mysteries Volume 2*?
Please consider rating it on Goodreads, Bookbub, or your favorite retailer. Reviews help me reach new readers.

This concludes the *Pine Grove Mysteries.*

Read all the stories
Jane and Kennedy Daniels Mysteries
Pine Grove Mysteries
Wilma Wade Holiday Mysteries
Mike and Maddie Mysteries
Mystic Moonhaven Mysteries
Annie Archer Paranormal Mysteries

Join my newsletter for writing updates, new releases, sales, giveaways and more!

ABOUT THE AUTHOR

Daisy Landish is a romance and contemporary fiction author living in the UK, whose clean and sweet novellas have tugged at readers' heart-strings across the pond and beyond. When she's not writing love stories, Daisy spends her time reading, hiking at dawn, and riding into the sunset on her horse, Rosebud.

Join Daisy's Newsletter for updates and giveaways!
www.daisylandishromance.com

f facebook.com/daisylandishromance
X x.com/daisy_landish
⊙ instagram.com/daisylandishbooks
a amazon.com/author/daisylandish
BB bookbub.com/authors/daisy-landish
g goodreads.com/Daisy_Landish

ALSO BY DAISY LANDISH

Clean Regency Romance

The Lady Series - The Allington Collection

The Lady Series - The Gillingham Collection

The Lady Series - The Blackmore Collection

The Lady Series - The Norrington Collection

Clean Contemporary Romance

Maplewood Grove Series

Love on Spruce Island

Second Chance

Cherry Tree Island

The Wedding Trio

Extra Credit

Counting on the Cowboy

Focusing on the Cowboy

Mistletoe Magic

Grounded at Christmas

Cozy Mysteries

Sophie Brooks Mysteries

Jane and Kennedy Daniels Mysteries

Pine Grove Mysteries

Annie Archer Paranormal Mysteries

Wilma Wade Holiday Mysteries

Mike and Maddie Mysteries

Mystic Moonhaven Mysteries

Sweater Weather: Cozy Mysteries for Fall

Summer Vibes: Cozy Mysteries for Summer

www.ingramcontent.com/pod-product-compliance
Lightning Source LLC
Chambersburg PA
CBHW020316260626
47156CB00004B/1242